THE SUMMER HOUSE

THE SUMMER HOUSE

(THE ROSE SISTERS, #2)

SIENNA CARR

AUTHOR'S NOTE

THE SUMMER HOUSE is the second book in THE ROSE SISTERS series which follows the lives of three sisters, Ashleigh, Eloise and Genevieve, who run The Bridal Shop, a family business.

THE BRIDAL SHOP is the first book and it told Ashleigh's story. THE SUMMER HOUSE is Eloise's story. While this can be read as a standalone, it is recommended that you read the books in order.

CHAPTER 1

"*A* week in Miami! I can't wait!" Eloise could imagine it now, spending time with her best friend, Beth, and her new husband, and some wonderful people she'd met at the wedding. "I *so* badly need a break."

"You sound tired," her friend Beth remarked.

"You have no idea." Eloise walked around the house with the phone to her ear, searching for Ginny. That girl was driving her insane. Her sister was still wallowing in pity two months after the wedding-that-was-never-to-be.

And thank goodness for that. Secretly, Eloise and Ashleigh, their older sister, were relieved that it had happened sooner rather than later.

Not marrying Ben Duckworth was a blessing, though it would take time for Ginny to realize this.

"Alex asked when you were arriving," Beth added, breezily, at the other end.

Eloise's heart jumped at the sound of the name. "He did?"

"Aren't the two of you in touch?" Beth asked.

"We were but then with Ginny's wedding plans falling

through ..." Eloise often reminisced about that blissful week when she'd gone to Beth's wedding.

Her friend had planned a plethora of bachelorette parties in the month leading up to her big day, but because of The Bridal Shop—the family business Eloise and her sisters ran—she hadn't been able to go to many of the events.

Instead, she'd gone to a couple of them, including the wedding, and she'd met Alex there. They'd had some fun, had flirted and gotten on well, and they'd swapped numbers and kept in touch. But their late-night phone conversations and text messages had dwindled to nothing as she and Ashleigh tried to deal with the fallout from Ginny canceling her wedding.

She'd lost touch with him, and now that things were slowly back to a weird normal—because Ashleigh was in Europe for four months—Eloise felt trapped, abandoned and miserable. She didn't want to be here. In charge of everything. Taking on responsibility.

She missed her interactions with Alex; the man had brightened her world for one glorious week. He was also the man she'd lied about to her sisters, when she'd pretended to be too ill to come home. She'd ended up staying with Beth for longer than she'd anticipated, but it was only a small white lie. She'd been ill for a day or two, not an entire week, as she'd told her sisters.

She didn't feel bad about it now, even though Ashleigh was jetting around Europe and had left Eloise and Ginny to take care of the business, but Ginny was as useless as an umbrella on a sunny day.

"Alex thinks you ghosted him."

Her friend's comment took her by surprise. "I didn't. We had to deal with Ginny." She'd been busy, and she'd sent him a text, when she'd gone a week without returning his calls and messages, because the drama around Ginny had taken up all their lives. When things had calmed down enough, she'd called Alex, then messaged him, but he'd ignored her.

She took that to mean that he had moved on.

"I explained, about Ginny," Beth continued. "And all the stress you were dealing with."

Beth mentioning that Alex had asked about her filled her insides with a girlish excitement. "He isn't with anyone?" She was feeling hopeful.

"He's still single. He got so excited when I told him you were coming to Miami."

"He was?" A burst of happiness exploded inside her and Eloise stopped for a moment, her hand on her heart.

Beth laughed. "The two of you were good together."

"We weren't exactly *together*. It was fun."

It felt so good to be wanted. She stuck her head through the living room, expecting to find Ginny on the sofa watching TV, again, but her sister was nowhere in sight.

"And you can have more fun in Miami." Beth proceeded to talk about the vacation, telling her the things she had planned. But Eloise's mind drifted to other things.

Urgent and more important things.

Ginny hadn't gone to work today, again, and Eloise had been left to take care of things. Thank goodness for their shop assistants, but this being the height of summer was a busy time for business. While Ginny's wedding plans had fallen through, countless other brides were still walking down the aisle.

There was plenty to do and she was still busy working away at the shop long after they closed. There were adjustments and alterations to be made on some dresses, and the accounts and admin still needed to be done daily. Eloise hadn't expected to be the only one dealing with things. Going from three sisters to one was difficult, and while the assistants helped a lot, there was still so much to be done. Their customers were easily irritated, picky, choosy, and had to be handled with care.

Brides-to-be weren't the easiest of customers.

But Ginny still didn't appear to show any signs of coming back full time, even though it had been a full two months since Ginny had canceled her wedding. She'd had enough time to whine and mope around.

Ashleigh had left two weeks ago and had urged Eloise to let Ginny work part-time hours for a while, but Ginny hadn't come to work at all. She was getting worse, not better, about accepting what had happened. She wasn't moving on and had become very quiet lately. Eloise was worried that she might be sinking into depression.

She hoped not.

She wasn't the right sister to deal with that. After a long honeymoon in the Caribbean, Beth and her husband had returned home but were finding it difficult to settle back into normal life. Normal life for Beth wasn't what others would call normal. Eloise fully expected her to end up being on a social committee organizing galas. Her husband came from a wealthy family and Beth would never have to work for a living. And now she'd arranged a vacation in Miami for all the friends to meet up again and was warbling on about the things they could do.

"What do you think?" Beth asked, at the end of her long monologue.

Eloise hadn't paid much attention. "It sounds … great! I can't wait." She wandered into the kitchen and surveyed the countertops and the stove, and her heart sank. There was nothing cooked in the kitchen. No signs of tonight's dinner. "She hasn't even made dinner. Oh, sweet Jesus." Eloise swiped a hand through her hair. "I miss Ash."

Beth laughed. "You miss your sister because there's no dinner?"

"I miss Ash because she kept it all together." It wasn't only that, but she missed her older sister for a whole heap of reasons and she'd only now fully understood how much Ash did for them all. She was the mother and father they'd never had, and the head of the household.

"Eloise, you poor thing," her friend commiserated. "Where's your sister at the moment?"

Eloise sat down at the small kitchen table and propped her legs onto an empty chair. "In Portugal, in the Algarve region, she said. I have no idea what that is. She says it's really pretty. We're due a video call this weekend and no doubt she will be gushing about her trip and all the places she visited."

"You sound bitter."

"I'm … not." Eloise coughed. "But she's left me holding the fort while she's off enjoying herself."

"Your sister deserves a rest," Beth pointed out.

"But she's left me with Ginny, who is useless at the moment."

"Ginny's heartbroken."

"No, she's useless. I mean, when a guy cheats on you, you pick yourself up and put yourself back together again."

"You're hard-hearted, Eloise."

"I've had to be." Because of her ex-husband's infidelity, she didn't allow herself to get close to people. It was only later, after they had divorced because he seemed to have changed, and they argued so much, that she discovered it was because her husband had been cheating on her. Unbeknownst to her at the time, he'd met with the younger sister of a college friend who was at their wedding. Her ex alleged that nothing had happened for months, but nothing should *ever* have happened.

The betrayal left a bitter taste in her stomach about men, marriage and trust.

Since then, Eloise liked to party. She liked to have fun without commitment—as she did with Alex, the man she'd met at Beth's wedding. Nothing had happened apart from a few kisses, but they had plans to meet again, and when he ignored her, even after she explained the reason for her silence, she was done with him.

But, an adventure in Miami was exactly what she needed, and if Alex happened to be there, then so be it.

She was allowed to frolic and have fun, and she could do that without allowing herself to get close and trust anyone. She certainly would never commit again. Men, as far as she was concerned, caused heartache, and Eloise's heart was not available to be broken.

"It's not that easy for your sister," Beth insisted. "I'm sure she needed the break."

Eloise flexed her fingers. Her stomach rumbled and she was turning hangry.

"If it's any consolation, Alex will be waiting for you."

"Hmmm." It was something to look forward to. With the way things were going, Eloise was in danger of being stranded in Whisper Falls, running the business her parents set up before their untimely and unexpected tragic deaths, and turning into a lonely old woman.

"I should go and let you make dinner," Beth said.

"I don't want to make dinner," Eloise growled. "I want to eat and go to bed. Today was a tough day. Come to think of it, the last few weeks have been hectic."

"You can let your hair down in Miami. All we're going to do is party and have fun."

Eloise rubbed her foot. Miami was too far to offer comfort right now. Sitting in the kitchen with her stomach screaming for food, and her feet sore from standing so many hours, she was miserable. "I feel trapped."

"Trapped?"

"What if Ash doesn't want to come back? What if she wants to travel some more? What if she gets the travel bug? What if she and Ford get together again?" It gave Eloise a headache thinking about it.

"You said they were together."

"I'm not so sure now. It looked promising but then Ash left. She didn't put her plans on hold for Ford; she said she'd already done that before and she was determined not to do it anymore."

"He might go and visit her," Beth suggested.

"Go to her? Whatever for? I don't think Ash would like that."

"But it would be so romantic," cooed Beth. "Their story already is, coming back and reconnecting so many years later."

"You think anything and everything is romantic, but I'm not sure there's been much of a reconnection. Besides, you're newly married. I'll ask you in a few years' time." She stopped herself. Just because her own marriage had failed didn't mean that Beth's would. "Sorry. I didn't mean that."

"I know you didn't."

"Ah, Miami! I cannot wait," said Eloise.

"Me, either. Coming back from our honeymoon and with nothing to do, I'm so bored already. Miami will be fun."

A huge smile lit up Eloise's face, penetrating to her insides. The weariness she'd felt as she'd walked back into the house after a long day at work soon disappeared after talking to her friend.

"Will Ginny be okay?" Beth asked. "You said she wasn't well."

"Ginny will be fine. She's only suffering from a serious bout of self-pity. She's wallowing in misery, but it's high time she got on with it. I had to get on with it when Ash left and she'll have to do the same."

"I agree. She needs to get over what happened. I can't wait to see you again."

"I can't wait to see you again," Eloise echoed. "I'll speak to you later. I'd better go and see what that sister of mine is up to. 'Bye."

She went upstairs and found Ginny lying in her bed. Eloise's insides hardened. She had a good mind to tell this spoiled younger sister to get up and get cooking. "Tell me that you managed to get out of bed at some point."

"I feel tired." Ginny's voice was weak. Eloise was poised in the doorway, arms folded, trying hard to not say anything with the anger that had built up inside her.

After a hard day, she'd been looking forward to having a cooked meal but it seemed that she'd even have to do that herself. "How long is this going to continue?" Even now, she and Ashleigh didn't refer to 'the wedding' because there hadn't been one.

"I'm getting better. I am. I promise I'll be back at work soon."

"You won't if you continue to wallow in self-pity, all day and every day." Eloise walked in and examined Ginny's face. Her sister was lying in bed. Dark circles under her eyes gave her a gaunt look. Guilt washed over Eloise. What if Ginny had been feeling low ever since Ashleigh left, and Eloise had been too angry to notice?

She felt bad for the disagreements that passed for their conversations these days. What if Ginny wasn't only sad about Ben, but was missing Ashleigh, too? Ash and Ginny were so much closer than Eloise and her younger sister had ever been.

Please, God. Make Ginny be okay.

Eloise was aware of her limits. She couldn't deal with a sick sister. She wasn't good at taking care of others, only herself, and she didn't have Ashleigh's empathy and compassion.

She would not be able to handle this.

"I wish I wasn't so weak. I know you think I'm feeling sorry for myself, but I can't shake the tiredness. I'll try and do better tomorrow."

Eloise pressed her lips together, searching for the right thing to say. "You did the right thing, Gin. He's better out of your life."

"Don't say that."

"B-but, it's the truth." She shouldn't have gone down this avenue. Ginny struggled to sit up. "Don't say that. I don't want to hear it."

Ashleigh would have said something wise and sensible. Eloise had to stop herself from launching into a verbal attack. She perched on the edge of the bed and moved a lock of hair away from Ginny's face. "You'll get over it, Ginny. There will be happier times ahead, I promise."

Her sister would find someone else.

Someone better.

She opened her mouth to say more but a knock at the door stopped her. "Who on earth can that be?" she muttered under her breath, rushing down the stairs.

She wasn't expecting any visitors. She was tired and hungry, and she had a sick child to tend to—because Ginny might as well have been one for all the help she'd been to her. And now this unwelcome visitor so late in the evening, only ratcheted up her grumpiness.

"I can't wait to get out of this place," she groaned to herself, a little too loudly perhaps because the tall and not-so-bad looking man on the other side of the door took a step back, surveyed the door number, then cast his eyes on her again.

"Is this a good time?"

He'd obviously heard her comment when she'd opened the door. "It is a good time," she countered.

He nodded. Then, "Eloise Rose?"

She scrutinized the man's face. Green eyes, dark hair and a beard. He wore a ball cap back to front, which he hastily removed. "Yes," she replied, blinking a few times, her heart starting to pitter patter. It was a feeling she hadn't had in years.

"Ford sent me. He said you wanted to have some work done on a property."

"The summer house."

He shrugged. "Ford told me it needed fixing up."

"Ah. Yes." The two-story house, which could be seen in the distance from the kitchen window of their house, was what Eloise called the 'summer house,' which she'd bought it with the proceeds of her divorce settlement. Back then she'd had ideas to renovate it and make it new and homey for her to move into. A home away from home, close enough to her sisters and yet her own living space. She'd check it a few times a month, to make sure no creatures had moved in, and that there were no leaks, and nothing had been broken. But as the years went on, the house started to look run down, aging with time.

With her eye on her future, she had reconsidered getting it done up and had mentioned it to Ford. He said he knew someone he could recommend.

This had to be that someone.

They stared at one another. When Ford had told her that he knew of a guy who owned a small construction company she'd expected someone old and wiry.

Not someone like this guy.

He looked like a baseball player. All big and gorgeous and sexy.

"You—*you* own the construction company?" she blurted out.

"Yes, ma'am."

She licked her lower lip. Even under his light beard she could tell he had a good, strong jawline.

Jawline.

Since when had she become a jawline connoisseur?

"And you are?"

"Liam. Liam Reynolds." Long fingers plucked out a business card from his pocket. He handed it to her.

"Ford Montgomery sent me. I'm sorry it's late, Ma'am, but I was passing by and I wondered if I could see the place."

"Now?"

"If that's okay, Ma'am."

"It's okay. Please don't call me 'ma'am'," she snapped. "I'm not that much older than you."

CHAPTER 2

"*T*hen what do you want me to call you?" the contractor asked.

"Call me Eloise." She tried hard not to gape at the wingspan of his shoulders while she'd been taking a guess at his age.

"Eloise? That's an unusual name, I mean that as a compliment."

"My parents had an affinity for pretty sounding names. My older sister is called Ashleigh, and my younger sister is called Genevieve."

"Sweet."

"Ford didn't say you'd be coming tonight." She led him out through the back yard, past the fence which bordered the expanse of fields. There, in the distance was the rundown house, her summer house, standing in the distance, overlooking the sea with its back to the family home. It looked like a lost lonely building, a bit like how she felt when she first returned to Whisper Falls after her divorce.

"Sorry about that. Like I said, I was in the area, and I wanted to swing by."

She didn't reply, feeling unnerved by the size of him. Not understanding why her stomach had gone all light and fluttery.

Alex, the man she'd met at Beth's wedding, had been in a smart suit, then a gorgeous tuxedo for the lavish wedding reception. He was polished and slick; tall, dark and handsome, too, and she'd noticed him immediately. The attraction was instant, but it was nothing compared to the way she felt around this rugged mountain man with his overabundance of hair and testosterone.

He was so unlike Alex, and so unlike her ex-husband, that she wondered for a moment if she might be ill. Maybe she'd caught whatever Ginny had. "Now's as good a time as any," she said, eyeing the house in the distance.

"How's that?"

"Just." She wasn't about to tell her plans to a guy she'd only just met. "Are you available?"

"Excuse me?"

The bright green of his irises held her captive for a few startling seconds. "F-for work," she managed to say, the neurons in her brain starting to fire.

"It depends on how much work is needed. I could maybe slot you in before a bigger project. Ford said you seemed pretty keen to get going with it."

"I am eager to get it fixed up."

The Masons, the elderly couple who lived there, had passed away and their son put the house up for sale. She'd purchased it with the money from her divorce settlement, with the intention of living there, but it had been too much of an effort to get the place renovated. As soon as she moved in with her sisters—for what was supposed to be a short-term stay—she started working in the family business and life got hectic. And, it was nice to be with her sisters again, after the last few months in a miserable marriage. What was supposed to have been a temporary move back into the family home, became something permanent.

When she started helping at the shop, she got so busy that she no longer checked on the house as much, and left it to languish and fall into disrepair.

It would be a beautiful place once she'd had it fixed up. It would be a good source of income for her and it would help fund her move to Boston which was only an hour away from Hyannis Port. She couldn't live in a small village again, hence the move to a big city made more sense. She needed to be somewhere fun and exciting, and Alex was nearby. Maybe things could develop between them. Beth said he seemed eager to see her. Whether anything developed with Alex, or not, Eloise figured she stood a better chance of having a more fulfilling future than if she stayed here and grew old alone.

Ginny would find someone else, and Ash would probably end up with Ford, if she played her cards right.

"Let me know what you think." But her heart sank as she opened the door and walked in to see the place in a shambles. She hadn't been here since the spring and now it looked more run down than before.

Liam removed his ball cap and coughed. "Dusty. Smells stale."

"I don't come in here much. I'm afraid I've let this place languish."

"How long have you had it?"

"I bought it a few years ago, with my divorce settlement."

He'd been running his hands down the falling plaster on the walls, but turned to face her just then. "I'm sorry to hear that."

"I'm not sorry." She wasn't going to elaborate.

He continued examining the place. There was no furniture here, just run down walls and interiors.

"I had plans to live here, but it got really comfortable being with my sisters so ..."

"And now? Not so comfortable?"

She didn't like that he could guess so accurately. That he could read her well.

"I'd like to do something with it, and not let my money go to waste. Maybe I can rent it out, or sell it."

"Hmm." He walked around, examining the walls the doors and windows. She cringed when his eyes slowly took in the damaged walls, Cracked and peeling paint with ugly stains. Loose floorboards. "You should let the air in. Open the windows. There's a lot of mold and mildew in here. It can be a health hazard."

She made a face. "I've not been good at that. I guess you can tell."

The fixtures were old and outdated, as if they were from another century, which, given that the Masons had been in their late nineties, was probably accurate. Liam ran his hands along the walls, assessing and examining. "It will clean up real nice when it's done. You've got the structure in place, doesn't appear to be too bad, given that it's been neglected for so long. Mind if I look upstairs?"

"Sure." She led the way and he followed. It had two bedrooms and a good-sized bathroom. He wandered around, examining each room carefully as she waited at the top of the stairs. Finally he returned to her. "You'd rent this out?"

"Believe it or not, some people actually come here in the summer months for vacation."

He raised a brow. "I believe it. People flock to Whisper Falls. I love this place."

"You can buy me out," she offered, half-joking.

"This has a lot of potential. It's a nice place. Small but cozy.

The views from here are stunning. Overlooking the ocean, too. It's really pretty. "

"Thank you." She wondered if he had a wife or a girlfriend, since he wanted a place that was small and cozy and had such pretty views.

She tried to get a glimpse of his ring finger but his hands were in the back pockets of his jeans. Once again he rubbed a hand over his beard, and looked pensive. She hazarded a guess at his age. Early thirties. Maybe.

"There's a fair bit of work involved."

She swiped a hand across the back of her neck. "I don't want to spend a lot of money on this. The idea is to make money from it."

"But at the same time you want to get it done properly…"

"All I need is for someone to fix this up for me, and fast."

"I can do that. The walls need plastering and painting, some of the floorboards will need to be replaced as will all the doors and windows. The wiring will probably need to be upgraded, and I'm guessing you'll want to have new fixtures and fittings."

She stared at him helplessly.

"You don't have water damage," he continued, "not that I can see so far, but I'll need to take a proper look."

"How about tomorrow, or another time?"

"Sure. I didn't mean now. I've taken up too much of your time."

"I have to make dinner."

"Sure."

CHAPTER 3

Ginny was making lunch and a wonderful aroma filled the house.

It had been a good week. After lots of moping around, Ginny had finally returned to work.

There was some color in her face now, but her eyes still had dark circles, and she still looked tired. Eloise continued to worry about her. She powered up her computer and glanced at her watch. "Let's see where Ash is today."

She was setting up to have a video conference call with Ashleigh, and she clicked on the link her sister had sent her. Like magic, Ashleigh appeared on the screen. She was sitting outside and behind her Eloise could see the sea. "Don't you look the picture of happiness," she said, sourly.

"Hey!" Ashleigh cried. "And thanks." She flashed a wide smile. It was a rare sight. Her sister hadn't looked this happy in a long time. She seemed relaxed, as if she didn't have a worry in the world. Her eyes were shining, she was smiling more. She had an aura about her. Like she was blossoming, like she'd gone from a withering flower to one full of life and energy.

Like she was happy at last.

"Hey!" Ginny came over and placed her hands on the chair, leaning over to get close to the laptop screen. "Hey, Ashleigh."

Ashleigh's expression changed. Worry filled her eyes. "You don't look too good." She sat forward and peered closer, her face filling up the screen.

Fear crept along Ashleigh's face. Gone was that instant glow that Eloise had just witnessed. She held up her palms, eager to placate Ashleigh. "She's been under the weather, but she's getting better. Aren't you, Gin?"

"She's sick." Ashleigh insisted.

"I'm getting better," Ginny replied. She sat down, folded her arms and leaned forward.

"This is *better*?" Ashleigh gave Eloise a questioning stare.

"I must have had a nasty virus. There's something going around, but I'm better now. I'm fine. I really am. You don't have to worry about me."

"Are you still hurting?" Ashleigh asked, probing deeper.

Ginny gave a nervous chuckle. "I'm not *too* sad."

"She's getting over it," Eloise added.

"I am." Ginny nodded as if to prove a point. "You don't have to worry about me."

"You don't look so well to me, Ginny."

Eloise shifted uneasily in her chair. She'd been doing her best to hold the fort, and she didn't like that Ginny's health had declined on her watch. "Where are you?" she asked, eager to change the subject.

"In Faro, in Portugal."

"That looks tasty. What are you eating?" Ginny sat forward to get a better look.

"Shrimp wrap with salad. It's delicious."

Eloise's mouth began to water. "You are so cruel."

Ashleigh grinned. "I wish you two were here."

"No you don't," Eloise shot back.

"Why didn't you take Ford with you?" Ginny asked.

Ashleigh opened her mouth then closed it again. Then, "Because this was my trip. For me."

"But aren't you together again?" Ginny persisted.

Ashleigh seemed to hesitate before replying. The weighted silence alarmed Eloise who, up until now, had considered that her sister and Ford were very much an item. Ford had been coming to the shop most days, now that she thought about it, and he always ended up talking about Ashleigh. From conversations with him, Eloise believed her sister and Ford were an item. She wondered if something had cooled down between them both. It would be a shame if that was the case, because Ford returning to his hometown, divorced, and getting back in touch with Ashleigh was the stuff of old romance movies.

"We are together, but we're not joined at the hip." Ashleigh tucked a lock of her hair behind her ear. "Just because Ford decided to come back to Whisper Falls, because he's divorced and wants to start over, doesn't mean I have to put my plans on hold."

"That's not what I mean," Ginny said quietly.

"You look good, Ash," Eloise noted, sensing Ashleigh's unease.

"You think so?"

"Yes, I do."

"Thanks. So, tell me, what have you two been up to?"

Eloise answered first. "It's been a good day. It's been a good week. Ginny finally returned to work."

Ash looked worried again. "I shouldn't have left so soon after everything that happened."

"It's not a problem. We're doing fine. Eloise is taking care of everything," Ginny said. Eloise glanced at her sister, quietly surprised that Ginny thought this of her. "Everything's fine.

We're fine," Ginny continued. Eloise sank back in her chair and it dawned on her that Ginny was saying this to make Ashleigh feel better.

"Are you sure?"

"Yes." Eloise and Ginny replied in unison.

"Look." Ginny turned the laptop around and angled it so that it was facing the stove. "I'm making lunch and everything's in hand. We haven't argued at all this week," Ginny said, as if the two sisters had accomplished a mean feat.

"No, we haven't," Eloise agreed. "And you left at the right time. Enjoy your trip and make the most of it because before you know it, you'll be back." She flashed Ashleigh a smile, expecting her sister to agree.

But Ashleigh said nothing.

Eloise waited with her breath hitching in her throat. She was about to say something when Ginny spoke up. "Eloise is going away and I'm going to be in charge. We've got this, Ashleigh, we—"

"Going away?" Ashleigh sat upright. Eloise tried to poke Ginny in the side gently, but her sister was sitting out of reach. "Going where?"

Eloise's stomach muscles clenched. She didn't want to lie to Ashleigh, and she'd planned to tell her the day before she left. "Beth invited me. We're going to Miami with some friends from the wedding."

Ashleigh raised an eyebrow. "For how long?"

"Not long."

"I'm perfectly capable of taking care of everything," Ginny insisted.

Ashleigh and Eloise locked eyes. "Is it wise to leave Ginny?" Ashleigh stared at her in quiet disbelief.

Ashleigh's question annoyed Eloise. "I wouldn't go if she was terribly ill. Will you stop acting like you're the one in charge? You're not here, Ash. You're on another continent. I've got this." Her words came out like bullets, maybe it was the guilt she carried over Ginny being ill, or the way her older sister looked at her, that made her feel guilty, but her temper flared.

"You're right." Ashleigh's brows pushed together, her expression not matching her words. "I need to stop mothering you both."

"You don't mother me," Eloise retorted. If anything, her sister mothered Ginny, but that was to be expected given that Ginny had been a toddler when they'd lost their parents.

Ashleigh's smile seemed forced. "I'm sorry. Go to Miami with your friends. I'm sure Ginny will be fine."

"I am going. I will," Eloise retorted, but inside she was irritated. "We're grown women and we can take care of ourselves and the business. You enjoy your trip."

"I will. I-uh …" Ashleigh's smile was weak, as if she wasn't sure how to frame her lips. "I wanted to ask you something …"

Eloise braced herself. "What?"

"If … it would be okay for me to extend my trip."

Eloise choked back a gasp. "Extend your trip?"

"She means she wants to stay for longer," Ginny explained.

"I know what she means," Eloise snapped.

"I don't have a problem with that." Ginny shrugged. She had the audacity to look at Eloise for approval. Eloise tried not to hyperventilate at the news and struggled to keep her voice level. "You've only been there a few weeks. How do you know already that you'll need more time?"

Her sister had planned a four-month vacation, and she'd only left three weeks ago, so how could she already ask for an extension? What was she *really* planning?

"I've met some wonderful people, and so many have said that I should also visit Greece."

Eloise arched an eyebrow. "And if they told you to go and jump into the sea, would you do that?"

Ginny's eyes widened.

Ashleigh turned quiet.

"What?" said Eloise, feeling like the outcast. "I was only trying to make a point."

"I don't understand what point you're trying to make," said Ginny. "Ash, you should visit Greece if that's what you want to do. You're already there, nearby, so it makes sense."

Ashleigh nodded. "It would be a shame to come all this way and not go there." Eloise slowly inhaled and exhaled, hoping and praying that Ashleigh would deliver the punchline; that any second now she'd laugh and say, 'I was joking!'

But the punch line didn't come.

"I've heard there are so many islands, and some of them sound beautiful," Ashleigh continued.

"Greece for how long?" Eloise asked quietly.

"Maybe an extra two weeks."

Breathe, Eloise told herself as she swiped a hand through her hair, and tried to calm herself down.

She and Ginny were always at loggerheads. Eloise kept her mouth shut. It would be bad if she objected to Ashleigh's plans. She'd only come out looking worse, and Ginny would be even more displeased with her.

"An extra two weeks," Eloise echoed. "It's fine by me," she managed to say, with a reluctance she couldn't shake.

"Take as long as you want," Ginny said. "Eloise and I are going to be fine. She's going to meet her new man soon, so she can hardly complain."

Eloise's head turned so fast towards Ginny that she was in danger of pulling a muscle in her neck. "What new man?" she asked, at the same time Ashleigh did.

"The one you met at Beth's wedding," Ginny answered calmly.

"You nosy little thing." Ginny had obviously overheard, or been eavesdropping. Eloise turned her back to the laptop screen, hiding her face from Ashleigh. She gave Ginny a cold stare.

"Who are you talking about?" Ashleigh asked, her voice growing shrill.

"Oh. Sorry. I didn't mean to interrupt…" It was a man's voice behind them.

Eloise jumped, the familiar voice sending goosebumps sprouting on her bare arms. She glanced over her shoulder to find Liam waiting by the door. She'd been so incensed by Ginny's 'mystery man' comment that she hadn't heard him walk in. And now he was patiently waiting in the doorway where Ash couldn't see him, but had obviously heard him.

"Is Ford there?" Ashleigh asked.

Ginny giggled. "It's not Ford."

Damn it.

Eloise peered closer to the screen and hissed "I'll tell you later," before getting up and walking over to Liam. She heard only the tail end of Ginny's explanation to Ashleigh.

"If this isn't a good time, I can come back," Liam said. He'd come by earlier to take a more detailed look at the house and she'd given him the key to let himself in.

"It's okay." But Eloise would have preferred if Ashleigh hadn't known a thing. She was still waiting for Liam's quote about how long it would take to do the renovation, and the cost, but she assumed a good portion of the work would have been completed by the time Ashleigh returned.

That Ashleigh had heard him was pure bad luck. Now her sister would want to know about Eloise's renovation plans, and she would wonder why Eloise was doing this now.

"I've had a good look all round and it's not as bad as I thought. You have no water damage, and the pipes seem to be in good shape. "

"Good." Maybe Liam and his crew would have finished on the summer house and it would be ready by the time Ashleigh returned. Eloise's hopes lifted.

Eloise led him through the kitchen and out of the main door. "When can you give me an estimate of the cost and the time this will take?"

"In a few days' time."

That wasn't too bad. She nodded. "I look forward to receiving it."

She walked back into the kitchen, back to the video call.

Ashleigh jumped on her the moment Eloise came into view. "What work are you having done?"

"That old place she bought across the field," Ginny replied.

"The summer house? But why? Why now?" Ashleigh asked.

Eloise felt defensive. "Why not? It's been years. I had to do something before it fell apart."

"Are you going to move into it?" Ashleigh asked.

This was what Eloise had been dreading. The hundred and one questions. "I'm not sure," she lied. She didn't completely trust her sister. Ashleigh had suddenly announced one day that she was going on her travels. She'd been making plans secretly and silently, and not even the reappearance of her former lover, Ford Montgomery, had changed her mind.

CHAPTER 4

"What new man?" Eloise asked Ginny later. She was curious to know how much her sister knew.

"You can stop pretending that you don't know what I'm talking about." Ginny put the wooden spoon down and folded her arms.

Eloise's heart plummeted. Ginny knew.

"You don't have to lie to us—"

"I'm not lying," Eloise insisted.

"You told us you were ill, but you weren't. You were seeing your 'friend'."

Eloise squeezed her eyes shut momentarily and cursed the phone conversation she'd had with Beth, believing that Ginny was tucked up in bed and fast asleep. "I was ill," she retorted defensively. "That wasn't a lie."

Ginny shrugged. "It doesn't bother me. You're entitled to meet someone and be happy, but please don't lie about it."

Eloise opened her mouth to protest, but she couldn't defend herself. Ginny was right.

"What's his name?"

"I don't want to talk about it."

"But you're going to see him." Ginny didn't let up.

"I'm going to see Beth and catch up with her after the wedding and their honeymoon. There are other friends. It's not the romantic encounter you think it is."

"You could have been nicer to Ashleigh about her wanting to extend her trip," Ginny said, a sulky tone hardening her voice.

"I was nice about it. I told her she could, didn't I?"

"You didn't sound like you meant it."

Ginny adored Ashleigh and she would stick up for her no matter what. "I was enthusiastic," Eloise countered. "I was happy for her."

"Didn't sound like it to me."

"You're imagining things."

"You're selfish."

Eloise jolted back, feeling hurt. The eighteen-year age gap between Ashleigh and Ginny, and the fact that Ginny had only been a toddler when their parents had died, meant that Ashleigh was often softer with her. Ginny seemed to favor her more. "Is that what you think? I'm doing my best, just like you are. I'm glad you're back at work now. You being at home has been difficult for me, with Ash away." She started setting the plates on the table and tried to avoid getting reeled into another argument. Ginny could be a whiny brat at times and she liked wallowing in her vat of self-pity.

"You're so callous. I'm making dinner. Can't you be grateful?"

Callous?

Eloise took offense to this, but she kept her frustrations to herself. They ate their meal in silence, and afterwards Eloise cleared up while Ginny stormed off in a huff.

The next day Ginny didn't come to work, complaining of

feeling ill again. Eloise rolled her eyes and went to work alone, grateful for her assistants. An important socialite was coming for a dress fitting and it made Eloise nervous to not have Ashleigh around for backup. She was alone and the face of the family business for now, and she would have to do her best.

Eleanor de Freitas, the daughter of a wealthy investment banker from New York, was coming for her last fitting. Eloise had done the final adjustments, but Eleanor could be picky, and difficult, worse, her parents fussed over her, pandering to her every whim.

With customers like this, Eloise usually hovered in the background, letting Ashleigh deal with them, but there was no place to hide today.

Miraculously, the visit went well. The dress fitted perfectly and Eleanor and her parents were happy. The bride-to-be was in love with her dress and her parents' eyes filled with tears as their daughter tried it on to show them.

Eloise breathed a sigh of relief when the family left. She had alterations to do on a few other dresses and stayed behind after the shop had closed. When she'd finished her work, she sat back and surveyed the empty shop.

Where dreams begin.

She surveyed the words in cursive gold lettering on the wall. This could not be her life. This wasn't what she wanted to be doing in her seventies and eighties, let alone in her late fifties and sixties.

She didn't want to be a lonely old woman overseeing the business, watching young women start their journeys to married life and more.

Where dreams begin.

She was going to leave Whisper Falls, and The Bridal Shop, it was only a matter of things working out; the transformation of the summer house and Ashleigh returning from her travels. Then Eloise would make her great escape.

For now it was her duty to stay and keep an eye on the business and her sister who was nursing a broken heart and, thankfully, nothing more than that.

~

Eloise woke up the next day and got ready to go to work but as she closed the door to her bedroom and made her way downstairs, she heard what sounded like Ginny being sick.

Worried, Eloise rushed to the bathroom and knocked on the door. When Ginny didn't reply, but groaned in response, Eloise yanked the door wide open. "What the-" She had to put her hand over her nose because the pungent smell of vomit assaulted her senses.

Ginny was throwing up violently into the toilet bowl. Eloise crouched down beside her, pulling her hair back away from her face, rolling it into a ponytail. "What's going on, Gin?" she asked, tenderly, even though she was worried.

Ginny wiped her mouth with the back of her hand, before taking a deep breath. She sniffled, then pulled the toilet seat down and did the flush. "Your fish pie," Ginny replied, her voice hoarse and crackly. Her face was pale, her eyes haggard.

Eloise was taken aback. "I ate it," she retorted. "And I'm fine."

"That's because you have the constitution of a horse," Ginny said quietly, sitting on the floor and leaning against the bathtub.

Something tugged at Eloise's heart strings. "You don't look well. This has been going on for too long." She'd assumed her sister was low after her wedding cancellation, and breaking up with Ben, from the whole drama of the situation, but something didn't feel right. Ginny had never been this ill before, and there was nothing wrong with her fish pie. She stood up. "I'm going to call the doctor."

"No. You can't."

Eloise was surprised by the anger in her sister's voice. "But you don't look so well."

"It's your fish pie," Ginny insisted.

"It wasn't that bad," Eloise shot back. But maybe her sister's immune system was so weak that she was getting physically ill from any little trigger.

"Please don't call the doctor. All I need is to rest a bit."

"You've been resting a lot," Eloise remarked. "It hasn't made a difference. You're not getting better."

"I will get better." Ginny's voice was a whisper.

Ginny was soft, and vulnerable, and she had been madly in love with the no-good idiot. This was going to take time, and Eloise would have to step up and stop complaining. "You're not coming to work at all. Not even for a day, until I say so."

"Don't call the doctor."

Eloise huffed loudly. "Okay, I won't."

"Promise?"

"I promise."

Ginny had a broken heart, and that would take time to heal.

CHAPTER 5

*E*loise struggled to focus when she got to work much later than usual.

She'd stayed by Ginny's side for an hour, before leaving her. Her sister being so ill worried her immensely and she often found herself wondering what Ashleigh would do.

What if there was something more wrong with Ginny, than a broken heart? A broken heart could be fixed, over time. She would give it another week before she demanded her sister go and see the doctor.

Though Ginny couldn't see it now, both Eloise and Ashleigh were convinced that after the stunt he'd pulled, their sister was so much better off without Ben. The guy was a jerk.

Work gave her something else to focus on and she was grateful for the distraction. When Darcie, Ashleigh's friend, called and asked her to meet for lunch at the diner, Eloise looked forward to seeing her.

Darcie wanted to know about Ashleigh, so Eloise told her about the recent video call and told her how good Ashleigh looked.

"That woman is having the vacation she truly deserves," Darcie stated. A twinge of jealousy coursed through Eloise's veins. Her trip to Miami was relatively short. What she wouldn't give to have four glorious months away exploring other countries. Anything, to get away from her current life. "Ash is going to extend her trip."

Darcie smiled. "She finally plucked up the courage to tell you?"

"You knew?" Eloise bolted upright, feeling defensive. "She only had to ask, nothing courageous about that."

"She didn't think it would be so easy."

"I don't bite." Eloise snapped. "Ginny and I are holding the fort just fine."

"I haven't seen Ginny around much," Darcie commented. "How's she doing?"

"She still has good and bad days," Eloise explained. "It's all been a big shock for her."

Darcie made an appropriately sad face. "Ginny was so looking forward to getting married. She was so fussy when it came to her wedding dress."

Eloise rolled her eyes. "The number of alterations we had to do. Every nice thing she saw on someone else's dress, she wanted us to adjust on hers accordingly."

"That's the price you pay for owning a bridal shop."

"Don't I know it. I don't know how Ashleigh does it," Eloise said.

"Does what?" Darcie asked.

"What's that about Ashleigh?" Eloise stared up at the tall figure of Ford Montgomery looking down at her expectantly.

"Your hearing is excellent," Darcie commented, drily. "Especially when Ashleigh's name is mentioned."

Ford pulled up a chair and sat down. "How is she?" he asked Eloise.

"I'd expect you to already know the answer to that. Don't you two speak to one another?" Eloise asked.

Ford smiled in return.

"Ooooh," Darcie cooed. "I bet they talk all the time, and he can't get enough of her."

Eloise sipped from her bottle of pop. "Asking me for more information is a little creepy, Ford." She liked Ford, she liked that Ashleigh had a spring in her walk ever since her first love had returned to the small town they'd all grown up in, but it surprised her when her sister didn't postpone her travels, or ask Ford to accompany her. The man was clearly pining for her.

"I don't mean to be creepy. I care about Ashleigh and I want the most up-to-date information. I miss her."

"She's talking about taking a few more weeks." Eloise watched carefully for his reaction. Ford's expression turned pensive. "She's entitled to." But he didn't sound too pleased about it, though.

"I have to go." Darcie got up. "This was nice. An impromptu catch up." She pointed her finger at Eloise. "Don't work too hard."

Eloise found herself sitting across the table from Ford. "So?" he asked, as she finished off her salad. She'd barely touched her French fries.

"So?" She frowned, waiting for him to elaborate. If all he was here for was to prod her for more information on her sister, she didn't have anything new to tell him.

"Liam tells me he's been over to see your other place."

"I'm waiting on his quotation."

"What do you think of him?"

For some inexplicable reason, the color started to heat her cheeks. She shrugged, wishing that Ford wouldn't stare at her so intently. "He seems okay. Seems to know what he's talking about. He comes highly recommended from you, and that's the only reason why I'm using him."

"He's a good worker, and he has a great team. He's going to try to accommodate you."

"How's that?"

"He seems to think he can get your work done in a few months. He said you were in a hurry. Are you?"

"I want to get the place renovated before it falls to pieces."

"Liam's the man to get things done." He winked at her before swiping a French fry from her plate.

Ginny was lying on the couch when Eloise returned from work, later that evening.

"Hey," she said, softly, walking over to the couch where Ginny lay, but Ginny's eyes were closed. Fear shot through Eloise's veins as she dropped to the floor and gently prodded her sister.

Thankfully, Ginny stirred and made a soft noise, before turning her head to the side. She seemed to be in a deep sleep. Eloise placed her finger on her sister's wrist, feeling for a pulse and sighed with relief when she felt the gentle beating. She fetched a blanket from the ottoman and put it over her before turning the TV off.

In the kitchen, she sat down at the table and slumped over, resting her face on her hands. She was so bone tired and she didn't feel in the mood to cook anything and decided to make a simple pasta dish, but first she had an important phone call to make.

She rang Beth's number as she put the pasta to boil. The Miami trip would have to be shortened.

"Hey! Are you ready?" Beth's excitement was palpable.

"I can't come for a week. I can only do a few days."

"What? Why?"

"It's Ginny. She's not feeling too great. I can't leave her."

"Yes you can. She's a grown woman. Unless it's terminal cancer, you should be good to leave her. What's a week, for crying out loud?"

Eloise startled at her friend's words. "Don't say things like that. I'm still coming, even if I can't come for as long."

"Alex can't wait to see you."

"You keep saying that, but I don't believe you. He hasn't contacted me."

"Have you contacted him?"

"I'm not going to. I explained why I went silent, and he ignored me."

"You play hard to get," Beth retorted.

"I don't get swept up easily."

"You did the last time," Beth reminded her. Eloise remembered how nice it had been to have someone pay her attention. It had been years since she'd felt the electric spark of attraction from an interested party. With her dark hair and hazel eyes, she turned heads, though she kept her guard up when approached. She was the tallest of the three sisters, though Ashleigh attracted plenty of attention due to her dirty blonde hair and hazel eyes, and Ginny was like a voluptuous goddess. "I was caught up in the moment. Your wedding was lavish. Like a fairy tale."

"You were attracted to him!"

"He wasn't bad looking. He looked good in a suit. After seeing guys in denim and lumberjack shirts, a gorgeous guy in a suit caught my eye. I'm only human."

"You said you wanted to be swept away from Whisper Falls," Beth reminded her. It was true.

She didn't want to be lumbered with the business and stuck

in a small town for the rest of her life. She was scared that Ashleigh would return from her travels and would want to do it even more, or she would be happy to settle down with Ford, leaving Eloise to look after the business.

But that was then. Now things were different. She was in charge. "I'll come, but more because I want to see you, than anything else."

"For the week?"

"For as long as I can." Though, if Ginny got worse in the next week, Eloise would cancel her trip.

"I guess that's better than nothing."

CHAPTER 6

Miraculously, Ginny perked up over the following week and Eloise felt more confident about leaving her.

Any thoughts she had of canceling her trip were soon forgotten and she was excited to go to Miami.

Beth, as usual, had arranged everything right down to the last detail. Her father owned a mansion there which was large enough to accommodate the group of ten friends. She was buoyed up by the idea of having cocktails by the pool, of being surrounded by friends and having fun. Of not having to look after Ginny, or worry about her, of not having to deal with persnickety brides and their equally persnickety parents. Of not being bound and trapped and worn down by life.

She had planned to go into work early today, and then Ginny would turn up a few hours later, and Eloise would leave for the airport from there.

She'd be in Miami by late afternoon.

"I'm going, Gin! I'll see you at the shop," she called upstairs, for once excited about getting to work.

"See you later!" Ginny called. Eloise opened the door and

jumped, when she saw Liam standing on the other side of it, his dark blue and black checked lumberjack shirt open, displaying a white T-shirt underneath.

"You scared me," she said, trying to move her gaze away from his beard. It wasn't a thick beard, more like a couple of days' growth. But it gave him a rough and rugged manliness which surprised her as much as it appealed to her. Alex was the opposite.

"I didn't mean to. I was about to knock." He surveyed her with amusement.

This man standing in front of her, the type of guy she claimed to have sworn off of, was responsible for the heart palpitations she was suddenly experiencing.

"You must have sensed I was here."

Did she detect a note of flirtation? She wasn't sure. "You're lucky to catch me," she huffed. "I'm going to Miami for a short vacation and ..." She was rambling and stopped herself, because Liam fell silent, as if he wanted her to continue with her rambling.

"Did you want to see the property again?" she asked, trying to figure out what he was doing here so early.

"I came to give you the quotation."

He'd come to personally deliver the quotation. "You should have emailed it to me," she said, trying to sound casual.

"I did."

"You did?"

He nodded. "Almost a week ago, but you hadn't even read it."

"How would you know that?"

"Because I put a read receipt on it. It lets me know when you've read it."

"Sneaky."

He shrugged. "It's useful. I knew you hadn't read it so I decided to come over and hand it to you."

"I see. It's been really busy lately..."

"It's okay. You don't have to explain."

"I don't want you to think I was being lazy."

Her cheeks felt like they were on fire. What a thing to say!

"Lazy? Why would you care what I think?" Amusement danced in his eyes. It unnerved her. She placed a hand on the side of her neck, feeling hot and uneasy. Why did it matter what he thought of her?

She didn't answer him, because she didn't know how to. She didn't want to explain what was spinning around in her head. This was all... so not her.

She'd lost the ability to be rational and sane.

Maybe she was coming down with the same virus that Ginny had had.

"It's not important. I've been very busy, and as you can probably tell, I'm not thinking straight."

He looked at her, saying nothing, making her feel even more out of sorts. "Let me have it then." She held out her hand and he gave her an envelope.

"It will explain the scope of the work, and cost of labor and materials, and the payment terms."

"Thank you." She would open it and read it later.

"If you decide to proceed, I can get started immediately. I had another customer postpone the work on their house, so I have a free slot available."

"Do I get a discount with that free slot?" she asked, feeling bold.

His brow furrowed. "I'm doing you a favor by not making you wait."

"I'm doing you a favor by having a project for you to work on," she countered.

He seemed confused by her logic. "I'm ... I have a long list of customers. There's no shortage of work for me."

"I'm sure there isn't." He was obviously very confident, and she now felt foolish.

His gaze fell on her suitcase. "Miami, huh?"

"Yes."

"Have a nice time," he said.

"Thank you."

"Will you get back to me as soon as possible? It can wait until after your trip."

"Yes. I will."

"Because if the budget doesn't suit you and you don't want to proceed, I have other projects I can take on."

He was probably going to charge her an astronomical rate, and now he was putting pressure on her to let him know quickly. "You're in great demand, I get it. I'll let you know soon."

"Appreciate it." He nodded. "Have a great trip."

"Thank you."

She closed the door and fanned the envelope in front of her face, while praying that her face wasn't red. She had never had such a reaction to anyone. Not since she'd met her ex-husband.

Don't even go there.

When she had calmed down, she strained her ears for sounds of what Ginny was up to, but she didn't hear the electric toothbrush buzzing, nor the sound of the shower.

Had she gone back to bed again?

Eloise's heart dipped with disappointment. She needed Ginny to start getting ready and to be at work in the next hour, at least, especially because she was going to leave at noon to catch a flight to Miami.

She'd even told Ginny of her plans last night over dinner. Deciding to remind her again of the timings, she went upstairs.

The door to Ginny's bedroom was open, and she was standing in front of her full-length mirror, staring at her reflection. Then she turned to the side, staring at her side profile as she stroked her belly.

Ginny's stomach was slightly rounded.

Just slightly.

It wasn't so much the shape of it, but the way Ginny was running her hands over it.

Eloise stumbled backwards in shock, as if she'd been punched. The noise as she hit the wall caused Ginny to turn and gasp before she quickly pulled down her tank top over her stomach.

"I thought you'd gone," Ginny whispered, her face was drained of color. "I heard the door shut."

"Liam came t-to give me a qu-quote for the ..." Eloise's mind was flooded with thoughts. Ginny had been sick. She'd been vomiting. She'd blamed Eloise's fish pie but what if the reason for it had been something else?

Something like morning sickness.

She rushed to her sister's side. "You're pregnant, aren't you, Ginny? Aren't you?" The words were like marbles in her mouth, she struggled to sound coherent. Her eyes swept over Ginny's belly and, even though there was no big bump, now that she had her suspicions, it was obvious to see what Ginny had been so cleverly hiding.

Eloise's chest felt tight, as if it if was suddenly harder to breathe. The signs had been there all along. Ginny throwing up, looking pale, and gaunt, not sleeping.

Ashleigh would have known straight away, but Eloise had no clue. She'd failed her sister. She opened her mouth to say something but no words came out.

It was still slowly sinking in that her younger sister was going to have a baby. "So, this is what you've been hiding from me?" Eloise asked. Ginny quickly put her sweatshirt on, before sitting on her bed, her arms folded as she turned away.

Eloise sat beside her, then ran her hand gently through Ginny's hair. "I wish you'd told me," she said, softly, to the back of her sister's head. "Look at me, Ginny. Look at me. I won't bite. It's okay."

There was no way she could go to Miami now. She would have to tell Ashleigh and get her to come back, because she could not deal with this alone. "Ginny. I'm not leaving you. I'm not going to Miami."

At this Ginny spun around and faced her. "You have to go."

"I can't. Not with you like this."

"I'm having a baby, not chemotherapy."

Eloise winced. "This is how you announce your pregnancy?"

Ginny cradled her stomach with both hands, now that her secret was out and she didn't have to pretend to hide it. "It's hard to imagine that there's a baby inside me," she whispered.

"How did it happen?" Eloise asked, trying to think back, trying to estimate how far along Ginny was since her sister wasn't offering any answers.

"How do you think it happened?" Ginny cried, her eyes wide. "It happened the way these things usually happen."

Eloise considered her words around this delicate subject. "Weren't you being careful?"

"We were but ... we weren't careful enough." She burst into tears and Eloise immediately put her arms around her, enveloping her in a hug. "Don't worry. Don't worry. Everything's going to be fine."

But in her head, a riot of emotions crashed. Worry sparred with dread, and she felt paralyzed, not knowing what to do, how to handle it.

She'd tell Ashleigh immediately. This news was way too

big, and she couldn't deal with it alone. She needed her older sister to come back and sort things out. "We have to tell Ashleigh."

"No. No we don't. Don't you dare, Eloise."

Eloise stared at her sister who was clearly not thinking straight.

"I can't deal with this by myself."

"I'll deal with it. You don't have to do a thing."

"What do you mean I don't have to do a thing?" Eloise cried, incredulous.

"You can't handle this. You're always so used to burdening Ashleigh with everything."

Her indignation spiked. "That's not true!"

"You're panicking," Ginny said calmly, making Eloise feel even more paranoid and defensive. "If Ash were here, she'd know what to do, but you're going to be selfish again—"

"What?" The hurt cut deep. "Selfish again?" Eloise moved her hand away from Ginny's hair. An awkward silence mushroomed between them.

"You can't tell Ash to cut her trip short," Ginny insisted.

"I'm… I'm trying to do my best, Gin." She felt utterly wretched. Taking Ashleigh's place she'd seen how much she'd left on her sister's shoulders. She was slowly coming to understand. But she was trying to do her best.

"I can handle this by myself. You don't have to worry about me," Ginny said, making her feel even worse.

"You?"

"Yes, me. I'm better now. The morning sickness was in the first trimester. I feel better now and I can do my share of the work and help at the shop."

"You don't have to. Not now."

"I want to."

"Don't be so stubborn!" Eloise cried. "I didn't know you

were pregnant. I didn't know that was the reason why you weren't well."

"Promise me you won't tell Ashleigh."

Eloise remained tight-lipped. How were they going to deal with this? "When is the baby due?"

"In January. I'm three months pregnant."

"Only three months?" She felt relieved. Of course. It hadn't sunk in. Not that she knew much about pregnancy, but Ginny was starting her second trimester. That meant another six months before the baby was born. It would be January and Ashleigh would for sure be back by then. She wouldn't have to deal with this alone. She held Ginny's hand. "I wish you'd told me."

"I knew you wouldn't be able to cope which is why I didn't tell you for as long as I could. Go. Go to Miami. I don't care. I can handle this but don't you dare ruin Ash's vacation."

Ginny sounded so defiant, and her words circled around in Eloise's mind. Did her sister really think she was selfish and mean and unable to cope?

"There's no way I'm going to Miami. There's no way I'm leaving you alone. I'm going to take care of you, Ginny. We'll get through this. You're going to be fine. And from now on, we'll rely on the assistants more. I'll ask them to do more hours. But you're not coming to work—"

"I want to come to work."

"Have you seen the doctor?"

"Of course I've seen the doctor."

Silence fell again, the air full of so many questions Eloise wanted to ask, but didn't dare to, yet. But there was one burning question she needed the answer to. "What did Ben say?" Ginny's being pregnant with his child meant that her sister was tied to Ben forever. That even though she had managed to get him out of her life, this little slip of an accident meant that he was always going to be in their lives.

Ginny fidgeted with her hands. "He doesn't know."

"Ben doesn't know?" Eloise threw her hands into the air. "When are you going to tell him?"

"I don't know."

"You're going to have to tell him."

"Am I?"

"He deserves to know."

Ginny chewed her lower lip.

"I wish you'd told us as soon as you found out," Eloise said. "Why didn't you, Gin?"

"I didn't know how to." Ginny's voice was so low, so quiet. So filled with trepidation. "You were always so angry and annoyed with me for being so sick and I couldn't help it."

Eloise felt awful. "I'm sorry I was so nasty."

"You didn't know."

"I'm not going to Miami."

"Like I said, I'm only having a baby. I'm not sick."

"You've been sick."

"I used to be sick, but it's stopped. Go to Miami. I can take care of things. I won't be by myself. Rachel and May are there," Ginny countered.

"I'm not going at all." Eloise turned to her, her gaze dropping once more to her sister's bump. "I'm not going. I don't want to. I don't have the energy or the same enthusiasm for it."

The others would already have arrived, and she would feel like a latecomer to a holiday camp. An outsider. "I want to stay here with you and take care of you."

Ginny stood up. "Again, I'm pregnant, not sick."

"How will I have a good time? I won't. I'll be worried and thinking about you every minute."

"There you go again." Ginny moved away from her sister. "You always think of yourself."

"I'm thinking of you!"

"You only ever think of yourself!"

"I do not!" Eloise's face twisted at the accusation. And then she suddenly stopped. "I'm sorry. I'm sorry." She rushed to her sister's side and hugged her. "I'm still in shock that you kept this secret all to yourself."

"You wouldn't have understood."

"I…I would have." But a montage flashed through her mind of all the opportunities she'd missed. The signs she hadn't seen. Ginny being ill, and tired and sick and pale.

It was Ashleigh that Ginny missed. It was Ashleigh who would know what to do, especially in a situation like this, and it was Ashleigh who was not there.

CHAPTER 7

$\mathcal{E}$loise panicked and considered calling Ashleigh to break the shocking news, but she had promised Ginny that she wouldn't.

So she didn't. Also, given Ginny's opinion of her, the last thing Eloise wanted to do was make things worse between them.

Ginny hadn't wanted to talk about the matter further, and had gone to bed, leaving Eloise alone with her thoughts, unable to sleep much through the night. She was so not the right person to deal with this and she hadn't been able to sleep all night.

Ginny pregnant, with Ben's child, it was the worst thing that could have happened. So much could go wrong. Ben was a careless, irresponsible, cheating good for nothing.

Her sister deserved better.

Just when it seemed that Ginny had dodged a bullet and gotten rid of Ben forever, the situation had changed so unexpectedly and now he was bound forever to Ginny.

The fact that he didn't yet know gave Eloise time to figure out how to handle this. Ginny always wore baggy clothes, and her height would help hide the bump so that her pregnancy would remain a secret for a while, but it wouldn't be under wraps for too long. There would come a time when her pregnancy would be impossible to hide and everyone would know.

Eloise had to figure out a way to keep Darcie and Ford from finding out and telling Ashleigh. Ginny would be heavily pregnant by the time Ashleigh returned.

This major new twist in the sad story of Ginny's entanglement with Ben was too big a life event for Eloise to handle by herself. One thing was clear, her trip was canceled.

She wouldn't tell Ashleigh. This wasn't her news to broadcast to anyone. She'd let Ginny deal with that, but she would be the best sister Ginny could have. Her sister would be a single mother, but the baby would have two aunts who would spoil the child and love him or her as if it were their own.

It brought a smile to Eloise. Ashleigh wouldn't have children, and as for herself, children weren't on her radar, either. She would soon turn thirty-seven, and time was passing. It was too late for her, given that she was still pretty much single and the chances of her meeting Mr. Right were slim. Therefore, this child that would soon come into their family, would be immensely loved and cherished. Ginny would never be a single mother in the sense that she would struggle in bringing the child up.

Ginny would never be alone.

Her family would be there for her.

She jumped when Ford walked in.

"You look like you've seen a ghost," he said, walking into the shop.

"I was miles away." She'd been lost in thought again, like

she had been for most of the day, wondering and worrying about Ginny and her situation.

"Clearly you're not, miles away, I mean. Why aren't you in Miami?"

"I decided not to go."

Ford's brows pushed together in disbelief. "Decided? Why?"

She shrugged, trying to display a nonchalance she didn't feel. "Just."

"Just?" Ford stared at her in disbelief. "It's not like you to give up a good time."

Eloise forced herself to breathe out slowly. Her reputation clearly proceeded her. What with Ginny's accusations, and this, she hated that she was so misunderstood. She wasn't selfish. She was someone who liked to make the most of life. "I didn't want to leave Ginny with so much to worry about."

"Is she ill?"

"No." Eloise scrambled to find a way to steer Ford away from where the conversation was heading.

"She still broken hearted?"

"Who knows?"

Ford eyed her carefully, still not believing her. "But seriously, what are you doing here? I told Ashleigh you were going on your vacation."

"Well, I'm not."

"You're sore about something."

"I'm sick of people labeling me a party loving animal."

Ford chuckled. "I never called you an animal. Now, tell me. What's wrong?"

"Nothing is wrong?" She forced a small laugh. "Why do you think something is wrong?"

"Because this is out of character for you." He gestured towards her, cocking his head. "I've never known you to pick work over a vacation. From what Ashleigh tells me, you might as well live in Hyannis Port with your friend, the amount of time you spend there."

This was interesting. "Is that what Ashleigh told you?" Having one sister think of her as being lazy was bad enough, but for both to think she was a good time girl was… hurtful. "I'm in charge, and I've got to keep an eye on things."

"And Ginny couldn't do that?" Ford was fishing for news, and she worried that he might suspect something about Ginny's condition.

"We've had a lot of new clients; it's wedding season and things are always so hectic at this time of the year."

He laughed loudly at that. "They certainly are. Especially for you to give up your partying for anyone or anything."

"People change."

"They sure do."

CHAPTER 8

*B*en was the last person Eloise expected to see walk in.

She hadn't seen him for months, and the shock hit her like a cyclone. He was searching for Ginny, no doubt.

Her stomach hardened at the sight of him. She continued to fluff up the satin dress on the mannequin she had finished dressing and pretended not to see him. She wished he would quietly and quickly disappear. Turning her back to him she continued smoothing out the tulle skirt, and thanked the heavens that Ginny was at home today.

But her wish didn't come true. Ben didn't disappear. Instead he coughed lightly behind her. "Uh... Eloise..." *Cough, cough.*

She ground down on her teeth, her insides hollowing out at the prospect of having to face him. Steeling herself, she turned around. "Ben." It was an effort to say his name.

"I was looking for Ginny."

"Why?" There was no need for this man to be looking for Ginny.

But he's the father of her unborn child.

She should have been in Miami, sipping cocktails in a bar overlooking the sea, but instead she was dealing with things she would rather not have faced.

He stared at her with a dour face. "I wanted to see her."

That's what she feared. Also, why did he want to see her now? Why couldn't he call her, instead of turning up at the shop? She examined his face, looking for clues. "She doesn't want to see you."

His expression changed. He smiled. There was no love lost between them. Ben was aware that she and Ashleigh didn't like him much. "You sure about that?"

Eloise swallowed, shock landing like a fist in her throat. What had Ginny gone and done? Had she reached out to him already?

"She texted me." His smile widened. Eloise was so tempted to slap that smirk off his face. "She wanted to know how I was. I think she misses me."

Eloise pressed her lips together, finding it difficult to say nothing. Then, "She must have had a moment of madness."

He chortled and it infuriated her further. "You've never liked me, you or Ashleigh. You probably celebrated when the wedding fell through—"

"If you'd kept your zipper up and not messed around, if you'd been a decent fiancé to my sister, things might have worked out differently."

"Where is she?" he asked, ignoring her and looking around. Eloise glared at him. "She's not here."

"I'll go and see her at home then."

She jolted at his words. "You'll do no such thing." She couldn't stomach the idea of Ben turning up on their doorstep. Face to face with him, Ginny might cave. Might invite him in, might tell him everything. He would need to know, at some point, but not *now*. She hadn't yet considered how to navigate the next few months, especially with Ashleigh being away.

They glared at one another in an eyeball standoff. Eloise was determined not to be the first to look away.

"She texted me. She can text me again." He sauntered out of the shop, and Eloise let out the breath she'd been holding in.

~

"I won't be long." She was going to check in on Ginny at home. Check in to make sure that Ben wasn't there.

She grabbed her bag and car keys, and when May peered at her with concern, said, "I'm going home. I forgot something."

"Is Ginny okay?"

"Why? Why would you ask if Ginny's okay?" People were starting to suspect.

"She's not here. She hasn't been here much, and now you're going home," May explained calmly.

"She's coming in more regularly. She's fine. I don't want her overworking herself."

May nodded, but it was obvious that she didn't believe her. Even as Eloise walked away, she could feel May's disbelieving eyes on her.

She drove home, her eyes darting around for signs of Ben's car, but luckily there was nothing. By the time she got home, her anxiety spiked and her mood had worsened even more since she'd seen Ben and listened to his smarmy words.

The simmering anger she felt for Ginny had bubbled up, and she tried her best to push it back down, mindful of the way Ginny already saw her.

She opened the door and called out Ginny's name. As she closed the door, Ginny rushed towards her, her eyes widening with surprise. "What are you doing here?"

"Have you had any visitors?"

"What?"

"Visitors. Have you had any?"

"What? What's the matter with you?"

"Has Ben been here?"

"What?" Ginny's eyes turned round with shock. "No!"

"You contacted him. Why?" Eloise demanded.

Ginny let out a groan. "Have you come home to check up on me?"

"Answer me, Gin. Did you contact him?"

"What's it to you?"

She had. She so clearly had. "Why, Ginny. Why?"

"Why?" her sister shrieked back. "Because he's the father of my baby. What's wrong with you? Why are you here?"

"He came to the shop looking for you. He said you contacted him."

Ginny's glare softened. "And what if I did?"

"What if you did? He came to the shop, Ginny!" Eloise yelled, tired and worn out by the drama of the day.

"He's the father. He has every right to know, you said so yourself," Ginny yelled back.

Eloise wiped her hand over her face, her brain misting over, leaving her unable to explain herself. She'd told Ginny that Ben deserved to know, but him coming to the shop now had unnerved her and she was contradicting herself.

"I knew you wouldn't be able to deal with it," Ginny continued "You freak out at every little thing. You freak out because you don't know what to do. You don't know how to help, and all you do is make things worse."

A knock at the door prevented Eloise from replying. She hated that she and Ginny were yelling at one another. "I'm sorry," she whispered, feeling a failure. "I'm … sorry. I didn't mean to shout."

"But you did. You came home and you freaked out because Ben—the father of my child—came to the shop looking for me."

A second knock followed. Dread set in as she opened the door. She was ready for him, Ben. She yanked the door open, struggling to compose herself but the face staring back at her wasn't Ben.

It was Liam.

She felt a fluttering in her stomach, as Ginny marched upstairs. "H-Hi," she said, hoping that she looked decent.

"I saw your car." Liam hooked a thumb over his shoulder. "I wanted to hand this to you, because I know you don't read your emails."

If he was trying to be funny, she wasn't laughing. "Did you hear?"

"Pardon me?"

She wasn't sure if he was pretending to play ignorant, but she and Ginny had yelled and screamed out her secret.

If he'd heard, he was doing a good impression of playing dumb. "Why are you here?"

"I saw your car."

"As you've already explained, but *why* are you here?" Her stomach churned as she realized why. She had promised him she'd get back to him soon regarding the quotation he'd given her.

"I've revised the quotation I gave you. I've applied a discount."

"Discount?"

"You mentioned a deal the last time we spoke."

Oh, right. *Right.* "I remember."

"Well, I gave it to you."

She regarded him with suspicion. "Why?"

He shrugged.

"I don't..." She gesticulated with her hands, not wanting to be indebted to him. "I don't want to … to feel like I owe you."

He waved his hand dismissively. "I don't mean for you to feel that way. You're helping me."

CHAPTER 9

Ginny refused to come downstairs, saying she wasn't hungry, but Eloise didn't want her to go hungry.

Not now, knowing that she was eating for two, so she brought her dinner upstairs to her room, but Ginny turned her nose up at that. Eloise placed the plate by Ginny's bedside table and left.

She'd lost her own appetite, and skipped her evening meal, choosing instead to collapse on the couch and lament the sorry state of her life.

When her phone rang and she saw Beth's name on the caller ID, she grabbed it.

"Hey!" she cried, so happy to hear from her friend again. She closed her eyes and imagined everyone having a fun filled evening.

"We miss you!" Beth cried. "Are you sure you won't change your mind?"

"I can't, but, how's it going?"

"We're on a yacht."

"A yacht?" Eloise longed to be there and could imagine

herself there. She could smell the sea air, feel the wind in her hair. Taste the cocktails.

"Come!"

Eloise groaned. "Stop asking me. There's no way I can come."

"I wish Ginny would grow up!" Eloise pressed her lips together, feeling uneasy at her friend's comment.

"Come later, when she's better. We're staying here for a few weeks, not everyone, but we'll be here, me and Griffin. Don't you want to escape that hellhole and have some fun?"

Eloise pressed her fingers above the line of her eyebrow. "Believe me, I want nothing more than to escape this hellhole, but my hands are tied. I can't do it."

"Your sister is spoiled, and a pain and selfish," Beth said. Eloise winced knowing that she was partly responsible for Beth's impression of Ginny.

"She's not that spoiled, and she's had a hard time of things lately."

"She's a grown woman, and the wedding drama happened months ago. Can't she see she dodged a bullet? I don't see why you have to be at her beck and call."

"I'm not at her beck and call. Now's not a good time. I promise I'll come and see you soon."

Beth howled with laughter, but it was nothing to do with their conversation. Eloise heard a man's voice and laughter.

"I have to go!" Beth cried. "Try and come."

"I will." She knew she wouldn't, but it didn't matter what she said. Beth was busy having fun.

"She thinks I'm spoiled? And *hellhole*?"

Eloise jumped in her skin, her head snapping towards the door, to Ginny who was standing there glaring at her. "How long have you been spying on me?" she cried, not wanting to have another argument with her sister.

"Long enough to hear what you think of me and this place."

Eloise swiped a hand over her face, wishing this moment would disappear as if by magic. "Did you eat some dinner?"

"I told you I wasn't hungry."

Her gaze swept over Ginny from top to bottom, and she saw that her sister was dressed and ready to go out. "Where are you going?"

"Away from this *hellhole*," Ginny snapped and before Eloise could say a word, Ginny disappeared. The next thing Eloise heard was the sound of the door slamming. She groaned, and covered her face with a cushion as she slid lower onto the couch.

CHAPTER 10

Ginny went out over the next few evenings and didn't have dinner at home.

She was polite enough to Eloise, and the two of them had breakfast together. Eloise was mindful of what she said to her, not wanting to provoke her by asking questions about her health. Ginny was in a delicate state, Eloise attributed part of her gloominess to missing Ashleigh more than ever.

Nothing Eloise said or did seemed to help. At least Ginny wasn't being sick anymore.

On the weekend, they had another video call with Ashleigh. When their video call connected, Ashleigh appeared even more gorgeous than the last time. She was tanned, her hair seemed to have caught the sun and was more golden, almost blonde in places. She was wearing a bright yellow dress, which only accentuated her tan even more, especially against the background of shimmering turquoise water and several large yachts.

"Where are you now?" Eloise asked, sitting forward, absorbing the wonderful scene of freedom and bliss in front of her. It was nothing like her world.

"You look so beautiful," Ginny squealed. "Are those highlights in your hair?" Jealous pierced Eloise. There was a lightness, and love in Ginny's voice when she spoke to Ashleigh, which was altogether missing when she spoke to Eloise.

Ashleigh twirled her hair around her fingers and gave a disarming smile. "Highlights? No. It's the sun. It's so hot here. "

"The sea behind you looks stunning. I want to jump right in."

The two of them laughed and joked and talked as Eloise sat quietly. Ginny showered Ashleigh with compliments which she brushed off, giggling and comments such as, "You think so?" and "Oh really, you think this color suits me?"

Eloise stared at her hands in her lap.

"You okay, Eloise?" Ashleigh asked, and the room fell silent. Ginny's laughter screeched to a halt.

Eloise lifted her head. "Yes. I'm fine." She forced a smile. "I was listening to you both, and I agree. You look fabulous, Ash. Where are you, again?"

"I'm in Spain!" Ashleigh gushed about the little town she was staying in and proceeded to tell them about the places she'd been to. They listened with interest as Ashleigh recounted her travels, and then when she stopped talking, it fell silent. Today's call was different from the last ones. There was a tension in the air which Eloise was eager to hide, but she wasn't succeeding.

"How are things at home?" Ashleigh asked, as if picking up on the unease.

"It's all good." Eloise flashed a megawatt smile. "It's good. Really good." Ashleigh had the instincts of a lioness when it came to her cubs, and she would soon sniff out the fact that all was not well in the Rose household. Thank goodness the Atlantic and the airwaves separated them.

Eloise yawned as if to prove a point. "I'm tired, but it's all good," she said, wanting to reassure her. "Ginny's been coming to work now and there's nothing we can't handle."

Ginny remained silent but looked at Ashleigh and smiled.

"So, what's next?" Eloise asked. They listened as Ashleigh reeled off her itinerary of places to visit next.

"I wish I could be there with you," Ginny said.

"Come!" Ashleigh lit up like a firework.

Ginny seemed to be considering it.

"Come!" Ashleigh insisted.

"I would love to, but this is your trip and—"

"That doesn't matter. I've had plenty of time on my own, and I would love for you to come. Maybe the vacation would give you a change of scenery."

Ginny gave a half smile. "Thanks, but it's okay. You enjoy your well-deserved break. We're having a ball here, aren't we, *sis*?"

"Wonderful," said Eloise, through a half-hearted smile as she balked at the sarcasm, though Ashleigh didn't seem to notice. Ginny never called her 'sis'.

"Are you two sure everything's okay back home?" Ashleigh's expression turned serious.

"Yes!" Eloise and Ginny cried out at the same time, as if they were both determined to convince Ashleigh.

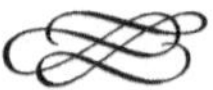

CHAPTER 11

Ginny started to come to work regularly, wearing baggy clothes and still managing to hide her pregnancy.

And she was starting to eat dinner at home, sometimes, though she mostly went out in the evenings, telling Eloise that she was spending time with her best friend, Talia.

A brittle awkwardness had sprung up between them, leaving Eloise at a loss as to how to act around her.

The Bridal Shop opened for one day on the weekend and was only closed on Sunday. Wanting to lessen the load for Ginny, Eloise offered to take on all the Saturday shifts. Usually the sisters had a rota for weekend work, and Ashleigh was the only who didn't complain.

One weekend, on her day off, she sat in the backyard to relax and was going through the digital photographs that Beth had sent from the Miami vacation. As Eloise pored over the pictures, her face dropped when she saw a photo of Alex with his arm around a woman's waist. She zoomed in, wanting to get a closer look, and it was clearly obvious that he was with her. "So much for being excited about me going," she grumbled to herself.

"Oh."

She turned around at the sound of Ginny's voice. They stared at one another for an awkward minute. Ginny was carrying a bowl of fruit in one hand and a book in the other.

"Were you going to read out here?" Eloise asked, as Ginny turned to leave. She got up. "Because I'm done… I was… I was going to see how the summer house is coming along."

She hadn't intended to, but now she would.

"Oh," said Ginny, again. "Are you sure?" Eloise waited for her sister to give a hint that it would be okay for the two of them to share this space. The table was big enough to accommodate six people, and the sisters had all sat out here many a time in the past.

But Ginny made no such offer. "You go ahead." Eloise smiled, even though she felt a sinking sadness well up inside her.

"Thanks." Ginny walked over and sat down, placing her book and fruit bowl on the table. Her baby bump seemed bigger. She guessed that Ginny was coming up to being four months pregnant. People would soon notice.

"How have the check-ups and baby appointments been?" she asked, tentatively. She'd wanted to be a part of this journey, had wanted to be there for Ginny every step of the way, but Ginny had insisted on going alone, taking Talia with her.

"They're going well. The baby's healthy. I'll get a scan picture at the next appointment. I can't wait to see it."

"A picture?" A rush of something warm and fuzzy filled Eloise's body. "Show me."

"I will."

"Are you sure you don't want me to come with you?"

Ginny rolled her lower lip between her teeth, as if she were considering. "It's okay. Talia's already offered."

"Okay, but if she lets you down…"

Ginny nodded.

"I'd better go and see what Liam and his team are doing with my place." She wandered off, letting out a huge exhale as she walked across the field to the summer house, grateful to have another place she could escape to.

She had the spare key, having given Liam the other one, so that he could come and go as he needed to. Ford had been over there a few times and had kept her updated, telling her that Liam's guys had made great progress, and the house was undergoing a huge transformation. But when she rounded the corner, and saw Liam's grey Ford Ranger truck outside, she was surprised.

The front door was wide open, and she walked in, blinking when she saw him. He had his back to her, and she couldn't help but notice, again, the wide span of his shoulders.

Rough and rugged.

Alex seemed like a pretty doll in comparison.

"You're working on the weekend?" she said, wanting to catch his attention because he seemed fixated on the plasterboard.

He turned around abruptly, then wiped his face with the back of his hand. "Why not? You do."

Her heart jumped. "How do you know?"

"Ford told me." He wiped his fingers with a dirty rag, and she wondered what else Ford might have told him. "Anything I can do for you?" he asked, his question making her feel like an outsider.

"I... I came to... to... "

Escape.

But she didn't voice her thoughts, for fear of what he might think.

"To get away?" She let out a gasp at his insightful remark, then saw him walk out before she could answer. She looked around helplessly, wondering at this new effect she'd acquired whereby people didn't want to be near her. But Liam reappeared, hooking a thumb over his shoulder. "I brought some chairs, so I could sit and have my lunch. You're welcome to sit out there if you want."

"What makes you think I didn't come over to see what you've been doing?" She walked out to see what he was referring to. "You have two chairs," she pointed out.

"In case I had company." He grinned and wiped his hands again. "Or did you want to look around the house?"

She didn't want to sit outside by herself. And it wasn't as if she'd brought her book to read, or anything. The last thing she wanted to do was be on her phone, looking at more of the photos Beth had sent from Miami. "I'll have a look around, thanks."

"I'll carry on with what I was doing, if you don't mind."

"I don't mind." She was relieved that he hadn't offered to give her a tour of the place. She felt like a teenager with a crush, instead of a woman in her late thirties who should know better about how to act in front of a guy she was attracted to.

"How's your sister?" he asked, out of the blue, prompting her to wonder how much of the argument he'd heard the other day. Plenty enough, judging by his question.

"She's good, she's fine. She was sitting out in the yard soaking up the sunshine."

"And that was why you came here?" he asked, turning his back to her. She couldn't gauge his expression, but once more she was surprised by his ability to read her so clearly. "Do you always ask so many questions?"

"This is a lonesome job, and I'm grateful for the company."

He was? Her insides jangled with joy. "You're in the wrong profession. You should have been a detective."

"A detective?" He chortled. "My parents believed that my

older brother was the smart one. They focused all their attention on him, got him tuition, paid for extra classes. He's now a doctor."

She felt sorry for him. "You were the ignored middle child, too?" she offered, thinking of her own story.

"I am a middle child, I have a younger sister, but I wouldn't say I was ignored. My parents weren't well off but, let's face it, who is? I was the sporty, boisterous one, and I liked having fun as opposed to having my nose in a book. My brother was the opposite of me and so my parents focused all their attention on him. Guess who's making the big bucks now?"

She wanted him to feel better about himself. "But you're your own boss. You have a team and your own company, and you can pick and choose what you work on."

"Don't feel sorry for me."

She stumbled back a step, surprised by his prickliness. She was only trying to help. "I—I'm not. I'm…. It's the truth…" She quickly changed the subject. "So, you're the only one working on this for now?"

"I have a team, but I use them as and when I need them. This is a small job compared to what I usually do. There's no rebuilding, there's no extending the place. I had the guys come in to fix the floorboards, and the walls needed replastering. This week I'll have them come in and replace the doors and windows, but I won't need them after that. Your walls will need painting but I can do that myself."

"Sure." She couldn't help but notice the way his muscles strained at his T-shirt when he reached up to the wall and ran his hand along it.

"Nice finish," he said, sweeping his hand through his thick hair, and causing her gaze to drift to his biceps again. "Did you want to take a tour of the house, or did you escape to get some peace and quiet?"

She was at a loss for what to reply, and slightly unnerved by his razor-sharp questioning. Was it possible that he had wire tapped this place and knew every word that she and Ginny said to one another? The idea was ridiculous, but Liam's observations were so accurate that it scared her.

She was annoyed because he could read her so well and she didn't have a handle on him.

"I wanted some peace and quiet." But it was obvious she wasn't going to get that here. "I should go. Ginny might need me."

He nodded.

She was aware that her comment didn't make any sense. Ginny wasn't a child, but she couldn't stay here a moment longer. The only thing left to do was to go back home and watch TV.

"Maybe you can take a look at the house on your next visit," he shouted after her.

She raised an arm in acknowledgment.

CHAPTER 12

Ford stepped out of the building with a satisfied smile.

The meeting with the bank manager had been productive and his plans to open an accountancy practice were going well, but his smile promptly faded when he looked across the street.

Ginny and Ben were talking and laughing as if they were old friends.

As if they were still together.

As if *he* hadn't gone and caused a scandal.

As if *she* hadn't canceled the wedding.

He stood and stared for longer than he should have, trying to figure out what to make of the scenario. It hadn't been that long ago that he'd seen Ben in a bar out of town with another woman. Granted that it was after the wedding had fallen through, but he'd been surprised to see how quickly the guy had rebounded from Ginny. But now this? Talking to Ginny again. Were they friends again? Why was Ginny laughing? Had she forgiven him? Ben said something and Ginny collapsed into a fit of giggles. He wished he could lip read.

When Ginny gazed at Ben, it reminded him of how Ashleigh often looked at him.

Ashleigh.

He'd lost her once, but now they'd found one another again, and he was damned if he'd let her get away again.

"Hey, Ford." He looked up to see Liam. "You seem preoccupied."

Ford nodded. "I had a good meeting with the bank manager."

"If that's your face after a good meeting, I dread to think what a bad meeting would do to you."

"Lots to think about." Lots. Maddie was in college, and his mom was ill. He was trying to make a future for himself and start over back in Whisper Falls. And with him and Ashleigh now dating again, he wasn't sure how that future would pan out. He knew what he wanted. The question was, what did Ashleigh want?

"Anything I can help with?" Liam offered.

Ford liked the guy. He'd used him to carry out some work at his mother's place over the years, and Liam had been good with his mom, and the quality of his work had been outstanding. They'd struck up a friendship and when Eloise had mentioned that she wanted someone to fix up the house she'd bought and neglected, Liam seemed like the best choice.

"I'm looking to buy a small office," Ford answered. He'd been looking for a while now.

"You're going ahead with setting up your practice around here?"

"Looks like it. If I need anything to be done, I'll let you know." He'd seen a few places he liked.

"Thanks. I appreciate the business."

"How's it going with Eloise?" Ford winked mischievously,

but Liam looked away, scratching his beard, pretending he hadn't heard.

"You'll be amazed by the house. It's coming along well. I needed to buy a couple of things from the hardware store."

"She doesn't know what a great piece of real estate she has, with those views and all that land." It was only from Ashleigh that he'd found out Eloise had bought it soon after returning home when her marriage fell through. It was only after Ashleigh explained how broken her sister had been, that he started to see Eloise in a new light. He'd known the Rose sisters decades ago, but then he'd left and moved away, and they'd become distant. Returning to Whisper Falls and finding Ashleigh meant reconnecting and rediscovering his relationships with them all over again. It was strange how the passing of time had affected everyone's lives, how events and circumstances had changed them all for better or for worse.

With new understanding, he saw through Eloise's hardened exterior. A guy like Liam might be a good thing for her.

"Is that Eloise's sister?" Liam asked, peering over Ford's shoulder. He'd seen them too.

"Shhh." Ford threw a casual glance in their direction, in case, by miraculous chance and bionic hearing, Ginny might have heard.

She hadn't. She was still dreamily looking into Ben's eyes.

This wasn't good. It wasn't good at all, and Ginny was being reckless to be seen with Ben. Eloise could walk past and see them. It wasn't unthinkable.

"Why the 'shhhh'?" Liam raised a brow as Ford walked away quickly. He followed. "It's Ginny, isn't it?"

When they were out of sight, having turned the corner, Ford stopped. "She's with that good-for-nothing."

"The one who cheated on her?"

"That's the one." Ford had explained it all to him before.

"Why's she back with him?"

"You think they're together?" Ford peeped around the corner, trying to see. He still couldn't tell. They were still talking, still laughing, but they weren't holding hands or anything. Maybe this was all it was.

"The guy she was going to marry, but didn't."

Liam looked thoughtful. "So, that's why they were arguing."

"Arguing?"

"It's nothing." Liam scratched his beard again and looked down at his shoes. Seemed like he didn't want to talk about it, seemed like he felt some sort of loyalty to the sisters. Ford needed to know. Ashleigh had asked him to keep an eye on her sisters, and this was a responsibility he took seriously.

"Can't be nothing if they were arguing in front of you." He knew from first-hand experience how hot headed the Rose girls could get, and the pressure of running a business didn't make things any easier.

"They weren't arguing in front of me," Liam replied. "I overheard, because I was at the door and they were loud. But not that loud."

If Liam was trying to underplay it, he wasn't doing a great job of it. "Don't mention that we saw Ginny with Ben," he warned. "Eloise won't like it and she's already dealing with a lot of things right now."

"Like what?" Liam asked.

"Huh?"

"What kind of things?"

Ford surveyed the diner and considered having one of their burgers for lunch. "Running the business and taking care of everything while Ashleigh is away." His stomach rumbled and he debated whether to have a double cheeseburger with a salad or with fries.

"Is she the one who usually runs it?"

"They all run it." He briefly considered asking Liam if he cared for some lunch but then remembered that he had to pick up some medicine for his mom. She would be waiting. He'd get a burger to go. "But Ashleigh is the oldest and she's always had most of the responsibility, ever since their parents died."

"That was tragic. You think you know heartache, but losing your parents at that age, is beyond cruel."

"It is indeed cruel. Life can be cruel sometimes. You know that more than most." A shadow crossed over Liam's face and Ford slapped him on the back gently, not wanting him to dwell in sadness. "Good to see you again."

"Come over some time and check out the house," Liam suggested.

"Will do. And, remember, don't mention anything to Eloise about seeing Ginny with that guy. Don't even ask Ginny about it."

"I won't. I don't get personal with the people I work for."

"We'll see about that," Ford murmured as he headed for the diner.

CHAPTER 13

$\mathcal{E}$loise peeped her head into the kitchen, anxious to see what was behind the loud sound of dishes clattering and clanging in the kitchen.

Her sister had her back to her, and Eloise couldn't see the expression on her face, but she could tell her mood.

Ginny wasn't happy. These days Ginny wasn't happy about much, even though she would soon be a mother.

Eloise's heart sank.

Ordinarily this would have been such amazing, happy news for them all—despite Ben being ignorant of the fact, and playing little or no part at all in the baby's life. Still, the birth of a baby, the next generation in their family, was a huge milestone and new life was to be celebrated.

But the good news had been tainted because Ginny didn't want to discuss anything with Eloise, and her attempts at starting a conversation about the baby often fell on deaf ears.

If Ashleigh had been here, things would have been so different. Ash would have known how to handle this.

But Eloise was trying. She'd given up her vacation in Miami, and was taking on the weekend shifts at the shop so that Ginny had her weekends free. Eloise was doing whatever she could to keep Ginny's workload light, and to be supportive, but Ginny didn't seem to appreciate anything Eloise did.

Being shut out of her sister's pregnancy hurt.

Today was a day off for them both, and Eloise hoped to get through to her sister, somehow. Ginny wiped her hands and Eloise ducked away, moving into the hallway and pretending to check for messages on her phone. Ginny sailed out of the kitchen and grabbed her keys from the side table. "Oh, I didn't realize you were here."

"You look nice," Eloise exclaimed as she noticed that Ginny had made an effort. Gone was the sweatshirt, and instead she wore a baggy orange top with jeans. Her baby bump was noticeable. "New clothes?"

"I can't fit into my normal ones, especially not the jeans. I can't do up the zipper or the buttons."

"Let's go shopping for maternity clothes," she suggested, feeling a pang of guilt that Ashleigh was completely in the dark about the big events back home.

"I have plans." The keys jangled in Ginny's hands, a signal of her impatience.

"Anything nice?" Eloise asked, a sensing of foreboding coming over her. Ginny was going out again. All week, most evenings, she was out.

"I'm going to watch a movie with Talia."

Eloise tried to force a laugh. "Talia sees more of you than I do."

"I see you every day."

"You see Talia every day."

"Why is that a problem for you?" Ginny's face twisted, and Eloise missed the sister she used to know. She'd take the spoiled, brattish sister that Ginny had been when she was preparing for her wedding, to the angry, irritated, sulky woman who looked at her with cold eyes daily.

"I don't have a problem, Gin. We never seem to talk or spend much time together outside the shop," she said quietly. "You're going to have a baby, and I'm so excited for you—"

"Are you?"

Eloise couldn't believe what she was hearing. "Yes, I am. Why wouldn't I be?"

Ginny sighed loudly. "I can't stand around talking to you all day. Talia's waiting for me."

"I'm worried about you. Are you seeing the obstetrician? Have you made your prenatal care appointments?

"I told you; I've got it all under control."

"I could go with you to your next appointment."

"Talia said she'd come."

The words hurt like a knife through her heart, but Eloise swallowed her hurt. "Good. As long as you've got someone."

Ginny opened the door. "I'll be back late." And when the door closed behind her, Eloise wondered what her sister meant by 'late.'

She glanced at her phone, wondering whether to call Ashleigh, because she longed for someone kind, and nice to talk to. Someone who wouldn't snap at her the way Ginny did.

But she couldn't remember where Ashleigh said she would be, and she wasn't sure of the time zone, and she didn't want another visual of her sister in a gorgeous location, not while she was feeling so down.

She had a free day, and normally this would have been enough reason for her to be grateful, but she was lonely, and she felt as if she'd failed Ginny at a time when her sister should have needed her the most.

She was about to walk into the living room and see what was on TV when the doorbell rang.

For a second her heart jumped inside her ribcage. Maybe Ginny regretted her words and came back to apologize. Maybe Ginny was ready to go shopping with her. She would treat her sister. She'd pay for whatever she wanted and maybe they could talk about converting one of the spare rooms into a nursery.

But Ginny also had the keys, and she wouldn't be ringing the doorbell. She rushed to open the door and jolted back in shock at the sight of Liam. "Hi?" The greeting came out as a question, and a small voice in her head wondered why he would knock on her door first instead of going directly to the summer house.

"We need to go shopping."

She tilted her head. An image of groceries appeared in her mind's eye. "Shopping?"

"For paint," he said, quickly. "You would be the best person to pick out the colors you want."

Go shopping for paint? *With Liam?*

"B-but... " She pressed her hands to her cheeks. "I have things to do."

"Like what?"

She scrambled to come up with a decent excuse. "I... I..." The thought flashed through her head again, and she wondered if he had somehow wiretapped her because it seemed eerie, how he knew she was free.

"Sounds to me like you don't have anything urgent to do."

It wasn't long before she was in Liam's truck, and he casually told her he was taking her to a home improvement store out of town.

She needed to get out more.

Who knew that traipsing around a large paint store could be

so much fun. After a couple of hours wandering around, she'd agreed on a few colors and had taken some sample pots of color to try out first. While there, Liam also picked up a few other things he needed for her house.

"That shade is going to come out dark and it's going to make your rooms appear smaller," Liam advised her when she picked out a lilac color.

"But it looks light on the can."

"Trust me. When each wall is painted, and they reflect off each other, the color will be darker."

She made a face.

"What about this?" he suggested, picking up a pale shade of blue, so pale that it might as well have been white.

"It's white. White is clinical. It reminds me of hospitals."

"This isn't white."

"It is."

"It isn't." He turned his cap around so that the flap was at the back, and she felt a pitter patter of something deep in her heart. Surely not attraction? It was only a ball cap. Not a bicep. He picked up the paint can. "Robin's Nest Egg Blue."

"That's a fancy sounding name."

"It's white with a hint of blue. It could be worth trying."

She happily followed him around, glad to be out of the house, and to be out, doing something. It didn't go unnoticed, the looks he attracted from other women. They would gape at him, and then at her, and she couldn't help but give them an he's-with-me smile in return, even though that was so far from the real truth.

That she could feel so happy indicated how lonely she was. Unlike her sisters, both of whom had best friends who were local, Eloise's best friend was Beth and she didn't live nearby.

It was yet another reason she wanted to move closer to her. Ginny had Talia and Ashleigh had Darcie. She had no one she could meet up with on the spur of the moment. And for a single girl, there was nothing like having a good friend on her doorstep. Of course, Boston was still over an hour's drive from Hyannis Port but it was much closer than being here.

This, going out with Liam to buy paint, was the breath of fresh air she'd needed, and she meant it when she asked him if he'd like to get something to eat.

"Eat?" he echoed, as if she'd asked him to marry her. It wasn't lost on her the way his cheeks colored, and how embarrassed he seemed for her.

How he was probably cringing inside, on her behalf.

She'd overstepped.

She'd taken this to be something it wasn't.

Not that she was asking him out on a date or anything, but having a bite to eat didn't signify anything, did it?

He obviously had a girlfriend.

"Oh. It's okay. Don't worry. I don't know why I said that." She turned away, humiliation burning her skin, and her insides imploding. All she needed was for the earth to open and swallow her and the disaster movie of a day would be complete.

"I—uh... I have to get back," he said, and the quickfire conversation they'd been having suddenly stopped.

She couldn't face him anymore, or the embarrassment he likely felt for her. Glancing away, she saw something that made her heart crash against her ribcage. She blinked, then blinked again. Time seemed to stop.

She saw Ben.

With Ginny.

And they were holding hands.

She blinked again, and they weren't holding hands.

Maybe she was seeing things.

She blinked again.

No, it most definitely was Ginny with Ben.

Not Ginny with Talia.

Eloise groaned, her chest sinking into her body, feeling as if she'd been hit by a car. What should she do?

"I have to get back, sorry," Liam said.

But she no longer cared about lunch. "It's okay. I need to go, too."

Before Ginny saw her.

She didn't want Ginny to find out that she knew her secret, that Ginny was lying to her.

She wasn't sure what she was going to do about it, but getting away from here was a good first step.

CHAPTER 14

Silence filled the truck as Liam drove her back.

She was grateful that Liam didn't try to make conversation. He seemed to understand her. Seemed to know when to talk, what to say, and when not to say anything.

Or maybe he was still embarrassed for her suggesting they get something to eat together. She wasn't sure what had possessed her. Maybe the sight of him in a red and black checked shirt with buttons opened and a white T-shirt underneath, might have done it.

Spending a few hours with him in a store, and having other women think that they were both together might have turned her head a little.

Eloise lowered her chin; the weight of worry making her head and shoulders heavy. This was too big a burden to carry. Not only was Ginny pregnant, but she and Ben were seemingly back together again.

She considered the consequences. Was it possible that Ginny was back with Ben? Maybe she'd reconnected with him, hopefully in a platonic way only, to tell him about the baby.

But if that was the case, then it didn't make sense for her

sister to lie. Why would Ginny tell her she'd gone to meet Talia?

"Something happen back there?" he asked, finally.

She turned towards him, her gaze fixing on his jawline. "Like what?" she asked, looking away.

He has a girlfriend.

"I don't know. You went quiet pretty quick."

"Nothing happened."

"Okay." He pulled up to the side of the summer house.

"You've brought me *here*?" She turned to him. "Why didn't you take me home?"

"I figured you might want to see what the colors look like on the wall. You know, test them out and all."

"You said you had to get back," she reminded him, an accusation in her words.

"I did." He turned the engine off and faced her, then turned his ball cap back the right way around, the brim hanging over his eyes like a shadow.

"You made it sound like—"

"Like?"

Like he had to get back to see his girlfriend or something. But she didn't say that.

"You said you had to get back, too," he reminded her, gently.

She pressed her lips together, not sure of what to say. She'd wanted to go home and process what she'd seen. She had a lot to think about; a lot to get mad about. Visions of Ginny with Ben had filled her head the entire time and she couldn't understand what her sister had done. She understood that Ben needed to know, but she felt uncomfortable with how comfortable they seemed around one another. Ginny seemed to have forgiven him and Eloise couldn't understand that.

"Are you daydreaming again?" Liam asked, climbing out of the truck.

She climbed out the passenger side and closed the door. "I wish I had the luxury of daydreaming."

He stared at her for longer than usual, and she wondered if she had a speck of dirt or something on her face.

"What?" she asked, her self-consciousness seeping through to the surface.

"I can see that you're upset." His tone was quiet, soft. She wasn't prepared for it. He pulled out the small samples of paint, as well as the other things he'd bought.

"I'm not upset," she lied.

She walked around admiring the new windows which immediately gave the home a clean and contemporary look. The living room was bare, but clean and fresh, as was the dining room. She couldn't wait to see what they would look like with a splash of paint and new furniture and furnishings. "You've done a great job," she said, in awe of how much the house was transformed. Only the kitchen and bathroom appeared outdated now, and odd compared to the rest of the house.

"Like I said before, most of the work is cosmetic. The wood needed sanding down, and varnishing, and a lick of paint now that the walls have been replastered."

"Mind if I go upstairs?" she asked, seeing that he'd sanded down the stairs and the old peeling paint was long gone.

He gestured with his hands. "It's your house."

She checked upstairs. Even though the rooms were bare and still unfinished, they looked new, they had potential and she couldn't wait to start brightening it up with new curtains and rugs and furniture. It would be a cozy home.

It would be hers.

"Like it?" She jumped at the sound of Liam's voice. It was rich, and low, and a flutter reverberated deep in her chest.

"It's coming along nicely," she said, placing her hand over her chest. "The kitchen and bathroom seem odd compared to the rest of it."

"I was going to mention that. It's up to you if you want to update them. I get good trade discounts on bathroom and kitchen fittings. If you want, think about it, and let me know."

She would need to. Getting the house redone but leaving those rooms untouched would be a mistake. Also, she was no longer sure about letting someone else have this home. She wasn't sure about a lot of things. "I'll think about it and let you know."

"Why don't you try these samples on the wall?" He opened the little cans of paint. She'd bought the Robin's Egg Nest Blue as well as a few others she'd liked.

"On the wall? Anywhere?"

"Anywhere. We're going to paint over it, so it doesn't matter." He left her to the painting, while he went downstairs to unpack the things he had bought.

After a few strokes of each color, she had to admit, Liam was right. The color he had suggested looked gorgeous. It wasn't white. It wasn't cold blue. It was pale and satiny, and fresh and clean, and not at all clinical, as she'd feared.

With the whole room painted this color, she could imagine the stunning view out of the window, especially in the summer, with beach roses, and black eyed Susans, the butterfly weed, sunflowers and petunias, not to forget the tulip trees which were majestically standing in the fields outside.

"Whoa." Liam returned, his eyes on the splotches of paint on the wall. "That's interesting."

"Interesting?"

He cupped his chin, taking a pensive stance. "What do you like?"

"It's obvious, isn't it?" She rolled her eyes. "You win. The color you picked is the best."

"You agree?" Once again, there was mischief in his eyes. She was held mesmerized for a few magical moments, staring into those sparkling green eyes.

"Yes, I agree," she said, pretending that it pained her to admit it. "You didn't need me to come along with you after all."

"Aren't you glad you did, even though you were so *busy*?" He lifted an eyebrow. She'd been found out. He knew she'd had no plans for the day. She was glad she'd gone with him, but at what cost?

Ignorance was bliss and she would rather have not known about Ginny and Ben.

At least not until Ashleigh was back.

The question was, *when* would Ashleigh come back?

"Thank you for today," she said.

"You're welcome."

"You can rush back to your girlfriend now," she said, feeling a twist of jealousy.

"My who?"

"You said you had to get back, earlier. I assumed you had someone to get back to." She swallowed, not quite believing the words that were coming out of her mouth. She'd been hurt too much to care now, and her curiosity forced her to question him.

To find out once and for all.

"I had to get back for ... for Lorna."

"Lorna?" *So, that was her name.* Eloise's body tensed in preparation. She fought to form a smile and failed.

"She's the mother of my girlfriend, Holly."

Her knees turned light and limp, as if her bones had turned hollow.

"She died four years ago from a rare form of kidney cancer."

She stumbled back a step, luckily hitting the plasterboard, instead of falling. Liam's words spun around her head as she tried to make sense of them. "I'm so sorry. I'm..." She felt foolish for having made her stupid statement in the first place.

"You weren't to know."

"I'm sorry. I'm so sorry for your loss."

He nodded. "Like I said, you weren't to know."

"I should get back, before I do or say something else stupid."

"It's okay. Don't beat yourself up about it. Like I said, you weren't to know."

She still felt stupid, and now couldn't wait to get out fast enough.

"I can drive you back."

"No need, thank you."

"I can walk you back."

"No, no. That's fine. Thank you. You should maybe go and see Lorna." She couldn't bring herself to look at him and was thankful to be walking home. The evening was still light, the sky peppered with gold and lilac. It would be the perfect backdrop for the long walk back to her house. It gave her time to think about how to act when she saw Ginny.

As she got near to her house, she could see that the lights were on. Ginny was back at home. Eloise inhaled a deep breath and turned the key in the lock.

A delicious aroma floated over from the kitchen. She prepared herself for the worst: Ben sitting at their dining table with Ginny, having dinner as though things were all back to normal.

She saw her cell phone on the small table in the hallway, and realized that she'd gone the whole day and not missed it at all.

Liam Reynolds had kept her quite distracted.

"You forgot your phone." Ginny's head popped out from the kitchen.

"I did." Eloise surveyed Ginny's face closely, knowing what she knew, and searching for signs of guilt or ... *something*.

But Ginny seemed calm.

Normal.

Innocent.

She disappeared into the kitchen, then shouted, "I've made dinner."

Eloise walked in, feeling hungry, especially since she hadn't had lunch.

"I've made crab cakes, with salad." Ginny announced proudly.

"You made them? You had time? Weren't you going to the movies with Talia?"

Ginny turned around. "I cheated. I bought them from the shop. Just had to pop them into the oven."

"How was the film?"

"Good."

"What did you watch?"

"Uh ... it was a romance."

"Oh, which one?"

"Uh ... 'Something To Hold'."

"Something To Hold?" Eloise repeated, making a mental note to check if it was playing at the cinema at the time Ginny was out.

"How was Talia?"

"Good. Sit down. I'll plate your food for you."

Taken aback by Ginny's offer, she sat down, as Ginny's lies needled her.

They ate dinner, making trivial small talk. It felt forced and on the surface, until Ginny said, "I'm going to tell Ben."

That's when Eloise almost choked on her crab cake. "About the baby?"

"Yes, about the baby."

"Can you forgive him?"

"I'm going to tell him about the baby."

"So you're not back ... you wouldn't ever consider going back with him, forgiving him?"

Ginny's eyes settled on her for the longest time, before she said, "He's the father, he has a right to know."

Her sister was too naïve. "It's just that, the trust has gone, don't you think? How could you ever trust him again?"

"I have to tell him."

She heard the edge in Ginny's voice and decided to back off. Today had been a day of shocks, and surprises. Her sister had cooked dinner, and wasn't hiding everything. Eloise hadn't expected Ginny to say a word about Ben, and while she hadn't told her the whole truth, she was telling her part of it, and she had to be thankful for that.

CHAPTER 15

It was almost midnight and she was in bed reading a book, but Ford was calling her, and it was another video call.

Ashleigh's heart leapt inside her ribcage, and she ran her hand through her unruly hair, hesitating to pick up. He usually texted before he called her, especially if it was a video call, to make sure she was decent.

She'd taken her makeup off, not that she wore much, but good under eye concealer and a light face cream with tint enhanced the gorgeous tan she had acquired and her complexion was much healthier now. She wouldn't look too bad, even at this time, without makeup.

She sat up in bed and answered the call, holding the phone in front of her. "Hi."

"Hey." Ford frowned. "You're going to bed so early?"

"It's midnight, Ford!" He surprised her because he was normally very good about the time zones.

"Is it?"

"Yes," she yawned.

"Are you still in Sardinia?" he asked.

"I'm in Sicily now. I got here a few hours ago."

"Ah, so you've been traveling, no wonder you're tired. What's Sicily like?"

"Gorgeous, like most of the places here." She knew what was coming next.

He cleared his throat. "Uh ... and where are you planning to travel to next?"

She'd already told him that she'd spent a week in Rome, and then had gone to Firenze, Perugia and Sardinia. She'd deliberately avoided the places they'd planned to visit on their trip, which never happened. They'd planned to go to Amalfi, Positano and Ravello, among other places. To have done that now would have been a kick in the teeth to Ford. He'd been sad when she'd stuck to her guns and gone ahead with her long trip. "Croatia is my next stop."

"Croatia? Where's that?"

"Across the Adriatic Sea from Italy, and sandwiched between Slovenia and Bosnia and Herzegovina." She hadn't known much about Europe before this trip, and she was proud of how much she had learned.

"You sound so knowledgeable."

"I've been reading a lot of maps and planning my weeks." She'd been doing that for a long time, when this idea of hers had been just a dream.

"That sounds amazing."

"I'm loving it. I could do this forever and never come back." That was how she felt. Out here, by herself, she was free and full of life.

Not tied down.

She was free to explore and to go on any adventure she desired. The travels had opened a new door for her and she'd seen and experienced new things, new people and new places. Sometimes she caught a sliver of what her new future could look like, and it was in these moments that Whisper Falls and the bridal boutique became a fragment of her past. She'd done her best with the shop. It was her parents' business, after all, but in throwing herself in it, wanting it to be a huge success—and it was—she'd lost a part of her.

But here, she ceased to be Ashleigh Rose, the responsible, cautious, and careful older sister.

She was a forty-three-year-old adventurer, explorer, a woman seeking enlightenment. She was meeting people from all walks of life, trying to get by with her broken phrases of the local language, wherever she was. Not having to live by a rigid timetable, not having to give up her weekend, not having to pander to fussy and particular brides-to-be who gave her so many problems—and they had every right to—but she was tired of it.

She didn't miss the accounting, or the getting up early, or the families coming to pick up the dresses and the brides-to-be having their dress fittings. She didn't miss the long list of alterations to be made and the constant pandering and taking care of everyone but herself.

But she did all these things with a smile and a weary heart.

She'd loved the shop once, but now it had taken too much of her, and it had not given as much back. Lately, the bridal shop hung over her head like a guillotine.

She'd watched doe-eyed women on the cusp of their married life, gaze adoringly at the words written in gold on the wall, their tagline, the quote almost every bride gushed on reading, thinking and believing with all her heart that getting married would be the start of a dream life: 'Where dreams begin' and she hated it even more.

Hate was too strong a word. She didn't hate her former life. But she didn't relish the idea of returning to it. Not after this long vacation.

"Never come back? Are you being serious?" Ford stared at her silently and she could almost see the cogs whirring away in his brain.

"Of course I'll come back. How can I not? But, I might extend the trip a little longer," she said, watching for his reaction. Now that they were dating again, she sensed that Ford was disappointed when she continued with her travel plans. He hadn't said as much, it was the expression on his face, the sadness in his eyes, which told her.

Maybe she was reading too much into it, but she wondered if he'd expected her to ask him to come along. They'd planned a trip like this all those decades ago when they were young and in love, before life had other plans for them.

Being with Ford was wonderful. Having someone to talk to, someone to share things with, someone to go to dinner with, someone to laugh with and commiserate with, it was fulfilling to have someone to share these things with.

To not be alone.

But there was a downside which perhaps so many years of being single had highlighted. She'd been her own woman for so long, and hadn't needed to report to anyone, or think of anyone, except her sisters, but that was different.

Being part of a couple meant having to answer to and explain your every move and decision to the other person. It was new to her and she wasn't comfortable with it. She'd had to do this with her sisters, but with sisters there were always squabbles and compromise.

With a partner, it was all so very different.

She felt hemmed in.

As if her wings had been clipped.

As if she was no longer footloose and fancy free.

Not that she had any intention of meeting anyone.

She was with Ford, and they were together. End of story.

Plenty of men had expressed an interest in her, but she had politely turned them down.

Still, it had been eye opening to receive compliments, to have validation where there previously hadn't been, that she, a woman in her forties, was attractive; that she wasn't a frump and life hadn't passed her by.

And now she wanted to extend her trip by another few weeks, something she had yet to run by her sisters, but she wondered how Ford would react. She felt selfish for asking for another extension, but it would be the last one. She wanted to be home by Thanksgiving. But she was out here, and some fellow travelers had urged her to visit Turkey. It didn't make sense to be here and not go. Who knew when she would next be able to come?

Ginny would be okay about it, but her gut told her that Eloise would have a problem. It had been hard enough for her the first time, but Ginny had been excited for her, and Eloise had calmed down after a while. It wasn't as if Ashleigh hadn't been working at all. Far from it; even being abroad, she'd been logging into the systems daily and keeping an eye on cashflow and orders as well as customer enquiries and emails.

The business was ticking along fine. She hoped that leaving her sister in charge had been a character building experience. She'd been to blame for taking on so many roles—mother, father, mentor, friend, counselor, sister, for standing in for them when they slacked off, and taking charge when her sisters fell short.

Having the space to think, and time that was not filled with a million micromanaged moments of things to do, she'd been able to take a step back and re-evaluate things, and she could see how she had enabled a lot of their behaviors. Eloise taking off at a moment's notice for yet another trip to see her best friend, or stay longer at her wedding. Eloise might as well move to Hyannis Port and live there. And Ginny, whom they had both pampered and spoiled and allowed to have free rein when it came to the wedding and the dress; it had backfired.

As the oldest sister Ashleigh should have been firmer and not let them get away with so much. She'd complained to Darcie many times, moaning about her life, but the truth was she'd enabled all of it.

If this trip had taught her anything, it was that she had to be more selfish. Think of herself more, instead of putting herself last. These thoughts rushed through her mind as she and Ford stared at one another.

"Extend?" he asked.

Even though a screen separated them, she could detect the hesitancy, the disapproval in his voice.

"I'm having a great time."

"That's ... that's good to hear," he answered slowly, and her ears picked up on every disapproving note in his voice. The warmth and affection that infused their video calls was lacking tonight.

"Do you think my sisters would mind?" she asked, mindful of the fact that she hadn't asked him how he might feel about it.

"Your sisters ... I guess you should call them and see how they feel about it." He scratched his nose, then sniffled.

She sat upright. "Is everything okay? Ginny? Eloise?"

He waved his hand with exaggeration, as if to show that everything was fine. "They're good. They're *really* good."

"And you?" The realization hit her like a tsunami. "Are you okay, Ford? How is your mom?"

"She's as good as can be, considering." He shrugged. "She's doing okay."

"That's good to hear. You look well."

"I miss you." The look he gave her, filled with longing and love, sent goosebumps tingling all over her body.

"I miss you. Sort of." As soon as the last two words escaped her mouth, she regretted them. But she didn't want to lie. She did miss him. She missed the way he held her, the way he kissed her, the way he looked at her with love and longing in his eyes.

She missed the new familiarity that came from meeting a man she had loved and lost more than twenty years ago, a man who had come back into her life again, professing his love for her.

New yet familiar.

But this vacation was a voyage of discovery. She was finding herself, somewhere in those layers of sadness and loss, and life, layers that had formed over time, with each experience adding another. She was peeling them back to discover the young woman she had once been, and Ford wasn't a part of this.

She missed him, but not in a way that he missed her, and it wasn't because she loved him any less—for she did love him—but what she'd said was true. She missed him. Sort of.

His face turned sad.

Oh my word.

What she didn't want was a needy man.

Please God, don't make Ford be a needy man. "Are you annoyed that I'm thinking of taking more time away?"

"I am. You were so worried before you left, about leaving Eloise and Ginny all alone to run the business, and you were fretting about Ginny after her wedding plans fell through—"

"But she's fine now. She wants me to enjoy my vacation."

"Yeah." He scratched his nose again, arousing her suspicions.

"Is there something that you're not telling me about?" she asked, her heart balancing on the edge of a precipice.

He broke out into a smile. "I miss you, but your sisters don't. They're enjoying their freedom."

"You make me sound like a prison guard."

"Are you implying that they're in a prison when you're around?"

She grinned, liking the easy banter. Everything was okay. Ford missed her. It was as simple as that. She wanted to soften her earlier words. "I miss you, and I want to be with you, but I need this time alone. I'm learning things about myself that I didn't know before."

"Like what?"

She gulped. "That I can be alone and not fall apart. That I'm independent, and I can fend for myself, that I am not afraid of messing up, of being wrong, of saying the wrong phrase in Spanish, or Portuguese, or Italian. That I can laugh at myself, not take myself too seriously, that life can be serious, but every once in a while it's okay to step off the hamster wheel and breathe."

"Whoa." Ford blinked a few times as if the words were sinking in. "You had to go abroad to learn all that? I could have told you how amazing and clever, and funny, and strong you are. You've always been the things you've newly discovered."

His gaze slowly inched over her face, as if he was seeing her for the first time, and her heart turned soft and gooey, leaving her at a loss for what to say. "I can see it. I can hear it in your voice. I can see the sparkle in your eyes. If you need more time, you take more time. The girls will be fine. "

"Promise me you'll still keep an eye on the girls."

"Always."

"And you'll tell me if anything's wrong?"

He smiled at her. "You worry too much. I love you."

"I love you." A burst of happiness surged through her. Being free to explore new places was wonderful, but knowing that the man she loved was waiting for her back home was priceless. "I love you, Ford. Whenever I think of home, I think of you."

Her words lit up his face and it was enough. Enough to know that the friction in their conversation had been soothed over.

"Promise me you'll keep an eye on the girls," Ashleigh begged.

The hazel in her eyes blazed through him and if he kept looking at her a moment longer, they would pierce the false front he had put up. The one that hid his worries.

"Always." He did keep an eye on them. He popped into the shop as often as he could, and he heard things from Liam, from time to time, as well.

He wasn't going to mention anything about Ginny and Ben to Eloise, because he couldn't be sure about his observations, but his conscience didn't sit right. He wanted to tell Ashleigh, but he couldn't. He didn't want to ruin her vacation.

"And you'll tell me if anything's wrong?" Ashleigh had asked.

He didn't want to lie, and he loved her too much to ruin this trip for her. He could already see how good it had been for her. "You worry too much. I love you."

"I love you."

She disconnected and disappeared, and he let out a long sigh.

He would have to keep a closer eye on the sisters.

Ginny could just have been talking to Ben. He hadn't seen signs of it being anything more than that. Maybe the two of them were making peace with the past, and moving on.

He hoped so, for all their sakes.

CHAPTER 16

Eloise couldn't function.

May and Rachel, the assistants, eyeballed her as if she'd dyed her hair bright orange. "Why don't you go?" May suggested.

Eloise stared at her blankly. "Go?"

"We told you to go home and that we'd lock up today. You must be coming down with something," Rachel said, softly.

Eloise considered the offer. "My head isn't in it today."

"Go home, Eloise. Go home," Rachel insisted. "You're working too hard. Even Ashleigh didn't do as many late nights as you've been doing. We can take care of things."

But she didn't want to go home. That's why she'd spent so many late nights here. She was on top of all the customer queries, the adjustments, the quotations, the emails with the supplies and designers.

All of it.

And now that she'd gone through the outstanding issues, there was nothing left to do, but the idea of going home repelled her. She couldn't look Ginny in the eyes properly after knowing how easily her sister had lied to her. She could handle Ginny not confiding in her about her pregnancy, but Ginny lying about Ben, *that* she couldn't handle.

"Are you sure you'll be okay to lock up?"

May raised an indignant eyebrow. "We've done it before. I'm sure we can manage now."

Eloise forced a smile, something she seemed to be doing on a regular basis. "Thank you."

She bumped into Ford as she walked out of the shop. "Hi," she said, wondering how he was always there, every week. She saw him more now than when Ashleigh had been here. "I don't have any news on Ash," she said, preempting his question.

"I haven't come here for news on Ashleigh," he countered, fixing her with a frown.

"Then why are you here?"

"You sound more grumpy than usual."

"I was about to leave," she protested.

"You, leaving work early? You're often the last one to leave, and you've worked so late into the evening."

"How would you know?" she asked, sensing that he and Darcie were spying on her and Ginny and reporting back to Ashleigh.

Ford laughed so loud she jumped. "I don't need spies. I drive past here and often see the lights on way past the time your sister used to work."

"Is there something you wanted to talk to me about?"

"Why don't I walk you to your car," he suggested, shoving his hands in his pockets and walking with her. She sensed Ford had something on his mind.

"Ginny went home early?" he asked, casually.

"I don't want her working too late. It's enough that she comes here daily. She's still trying to move on."

"Move on?" Ford asked, his question arousing her suspicions. Ginny was beginning to show and it was possible that people were starting to notice. Anxiety bubbled in her chest. Ford knew. It's why he was here, fishing for information.

She started to panic. The last thing she wanted was for this news to reach Ashleigh. She didn't want her sister to find out from Darcie or Ford. The news had to come from Ginny, and in person, when Ashleigh returned. The likelihood was that Ginny wouldn't have to say a word to Ashleigh. One look at Ginny and she'd soon know the truth.

"She's trying to get on with her life."

"She's not moping around the house like before?"

Eloise scoffed. "She's out most nights. She doesn't mope anymore, thank goodness. I call it progress."

"I hear you. It's a ... it's a good thing."

They reached her car and Eloise held back from unlocking the door. "It is."

"Yes, it is," said Ford, agreeing, but his robotic replies were sending her into a tailspin.

"Not long to go now," said Eloise.

"Until what?" Ford asked, clearing his throat.

"Until Ash comes back."

"No. It's not long at all," he said, starting to irritate her. He coughed lightly. But she panicked. Ford was being strange.

He knew.

He'd obviously seen Ginny and he'd found out. And now he was waiting for Eloise to say something.

"She's eating a lot at the moment," Eloise said, in an attempt to explain why Ginny looked bigger.

"Who is?"

"Ginny. She's eating a lot of junk food." Small white lies wouldn't hurt.

"Okaaay." He looked at her as if he had no idea why she was sharing this. Maybe he hadn't noticed. "Have you heard from Ash?" she asked, moving swiftly to a new topic.

"I spoke to her last night. She's having a great time. Told me that she'd found herself."

Eloise blinked. "Found herself?"

"Discovered who she was."

"Ahhh." Eloise nodded. Away from the daily life, away from her environment, she could see how her sister had the time and space to discover herself.

"I miss her," said Ford, a faraway look in his eyes.

"Aww, you lovebirds. You lovebirds who finally found one another again." She playfully poked him in the chest.

They were in love. She could see it in the way Ford's eyes turned all soft when he looked at Ashleigh. It was in the way he was around her, strong but romantic.

"Yeah." He looked away. He was a man of few words, though he probably wasn't like that with Ashleigh.

He didn't pour his feelings out to those he wasn't close to, like Liam. Liam had suddenly opened up. He'd gone from being brusque with her, almost standoffish, to wanting to take her shopping for paint.

It wasn't out of character. That's what other builders, or painters and handymen would have done.

Right?

Wrong.

This wasn't normal.

She'd been feeling unsettled, thinking that a guy like him would probably not be single, and then he'd opened up and told her about the girlfriend who had died. And he was still in touch with her mom.

The man had a good heart. A tender heart. But he might still be with someone. She was about say something when Ford started to talk about Ashleigh again.

"She's so happy; the happiest I've seen in a while, so if she wants to stay out there for a little longer—"

"She what?" Eloise asked, hoping she had misheard. "She has extended, because she wanted to visit ... Greece." She wasn't sure. She was losing track of all the places Ashleigh had gushed about.

"She also wants to go to Turkey."

"She ... she wants to take *more* time out?" This couldn't happen. Eloise was already at the end of her tether dealing with Ginny, and then there was the pregnancy, and Ben. There was only so much she could do, and if God forbid Ginny and Ben got together, Eloise couldn't handle that, not with the baby news on top of that, which, maybe, Ford hadn't yet noticed. And if he had, he was doing a really good job of pretending he didn't know.

"She said since she's already out there—"

"Then she might as well see it because what's the point of going back..." Eloise said, echoing Ashleigh's words. Her heart sank like a stone into the bottom of a river. Her body felt weighted with a new burden. "For how long?"

"Maybe a few weeks. Don't go being all mad at her. Just don't. Your sister needs this time to herself, so let her have it." Ford shrugged. "You girls seem to be doing fine without her."

The moment stretched out, pregnant with secrets that could not be told. "We are, aren't we?" She forced a small laugh. "We're doing fine. Fine. Fine. Fine." She paced around in front of him, thinking, wondering, fretting.

If her problems were only about the shop, and her and Ginny getting on, she could agree to Ash's new plan, but the situation was getting worse and Ashleigh was still in the dark about most of it.

She stared at Ford, and he must have seen a change in her because he stepped towards her. "What is it?"

She opened her mouth. The burden was too much. She couldn't bear it alone. Couldn't keep such news to herself.

Ginny was weak, and Ben, he could be controlling. He hadn't canceled the wedding, Ginny had.

Ginny would give in. She would let Ben into her life again. A man who cheated once was to never be trusted. She opened her mouth to tell Ford, felt as if she was on a cliff edge, about to jump off. "I can't wait for her to come back. I want someone to share the chores with again." She raised her hand dismissively. "I'm being selfish. It's fine. It's okay. Ash can stay for longer. I know how much she does, how much she's done." Having stepped into her sister's shoes, she had now seen it for herself. She would take care of things at home. She'd have to step up.

"That's good of you." Ford looked appreciative. Ash was lucky to have someone like Ford taking care of her and wanting the best for her. She hoped her sister appreciated him.

"Don't tell her I told you. Let her tell you herself," said Ford, as she opened the car door.

Secrets. More secrets.

"I won't say a word."

But as she drove back, she had no real desire to go home and considered going to the summer house to see how Liam was getting on with the painting. Then she decided against it, because it was easier to fight this friendly attraction which, for all she knew, was purely one-sided.

Instead she went home, only to find a scribbled message her sister had left on the kitchen table. Ginny had gone to Talia's for dinner, allegedly.

Lies, lies, and more lies.

She grabbed the back of the chair, her knuckles gripping the wooden slats hard, her head lowered as she closed her eyes and breathed in and out slowly a few times.

What would Ashleigh do if she were here?

If Ashleigh were here, Ginny wouldn't behave this way.

Ashleigh would smooth things over and everyone would be happy, and everything would be fine.

She didn't want to think about it. Didn't want to dwell on the problems in her life.

An idea went off in her head like a lightbulb. She would go to the summer house. Infuriated, she turned on her heels and left while rage simmered under her skin. She could better face Liam now.

She jumped into her car and drove over, not wanting to waste time walking.

The door was ajar, and she heard music playing. She stepped inside and stopped abruptly. Liam had his back to her and he was shirtless.

Her mouth watered; her knees turned weak. It happened so slowly. Time crawled to a halt, and she couldn't drag her gaze away. In awe, completely rooted to the floor, she stood there, gawking at his body. Lust coiled inside her, desire heated her skin.

She hadn't felt this rush of heady emotions in a while.

Not even with Alex.

Then, as she silently stared, he set his paint roller down, then reached for his T-shirt which lay on a chair. He lifted his arms, which made his biceps flex and caused ripples in the muscles along his back, before pulling the T-shirt over his head. She dropped her car keys, jaw open, and he spun around.

"I didn't know you were here." He rolled down his T-shirt, covering up his bare skin, and filling her with disappointment. She dragged her eyes to his, closed her mouth, and prayed that she wasn't drooling.

It must have been obvious, for him to see the want in her eyes, every cell in her body vibrating with joy. This animal magnetism that sparked between them—surely it wasn't one sided?

"I–I—uh." She shook her head, trying to clear the thick fog that had descended. Trying to string together a coherent sentence. "I finished early today, so ..."

"You want to help?" he suggested, holding out a roller for her.

Yes, yes, yes.

"Sure," she replied, with a calmness she didn't feel.

"Thanks. I could do with some help."

He hadn't even asked why she was here, or what she wanted.

Was it that obvious? Did she have some sort of sticky note on her forehead saying, "I'm lonely."

"But you'll get your clothes dirty." He reached out and touched the sleeve of her blouse. A touch which reverberated through her entire body. Was it her imagination or had he really touched her? "Is that ... is that why you t-took your T-shirt off?"

"I took it off because I was hot."

"Hot. Yes. It's been hot. The sun has been very hot today."

His lips pressed together as if he was doing his best to smother a smile.

"Don't worry about the blouse. I've got plenty more." She took a few steps away from him, because the heat between their bodies was becoming too much.

"Why don't you finish off this wall here?" he suggested, giving her the roller.

"Okay."

"I'll get another roller out of my truck."

She was relieved when he left, and took a big inhale. Her skin sizzled. Her heart hammered. She had never experienced this with Alex.

When Liam returned, they worked, listening to the radio, but otherwise in silence. He was in another room, and she was thankful for the distance for it gave her time and space to process her reaction to him.

Doing this—painting the wall, focusing on her strokes—gave her time to calm down and think.

It would be okay to let Ashleigh take more time.

It would be okay for Ben to know about the baby.

It was okay for her to be attracted to someone new.

CHAPTER 17

*E*loise no longer stayed at work as late as she had been doing.

She soon got used to the idea of going home early, and discovered that she loved the peace and quiet time to process things, because there was much to process.

Compared to her personal life, the business side of things was by far the easier to handle. It had become increasingly obvious to her that if she and Ginny pulled their weight, as they had been doing, Ashleigh's load could be lightened.

She liked going to the summer house in the evenings, excited by its transformation. She liked helping Liam. Liked being in a space where she didn't have to argue or be fed likes, like at home. He'd even brought her overalls, which he handed her one evening, because he didn't want her clothes to get dirty.

They were almost finished with painting the lower floor and would next start on the upstairs.

In getting to know him she was slowly discovering more about him, and found him to be kind and thoughtful, and attentive. Good looking and gorgeous. Whenever she stepped foot into the house, her pulse would race and her mind would turn all fuzzy.

Once the top floor was painted, and the staircase and doors were varnished, Liam's work on the house would be complete. She was worried that in helping him, his work would finish sooner, so she tried to go as slowly as she could. It would be better for her not to help him at all, but she looked forward to her evenings there, in his company. It was her time to relax and unwind, to get away from the stresses of her daily life.

One evening, they finished painting the last room downstairs and took a small break.

"Any plans for the weekend," she asked, wiping her hands. "Any plans to see Lorna?"

He seemed surprised at the question. "No."

"Any plans to see anyone or ... do anything?" she asked, feeling foolish now that the words were out in the open, not bats flying around in a cave.

"I'm going to come here, and work on your house. You?"

"I'm going to work."

"Six days?"

"We usually take it in turns to have days off in the week, and we alternate working on Saturdays, but with Ash not here, and Ginny ... well, with Ginny... I don't want to stress her out."

"You're doing a lot of days then coming here and working some more?"

She nodded, mesmerized by the rich tone of his voice. "I find it therapeutic."

"Painting, or talking to me?" he asked, his voice feeling like a low rumble in her chest, as if the words had penetrated deeper and had another meaning.

She laughed nervously.

He glanced at his watch. "I'm going to start upstairs."

"Now?" Her eyes widened. This late on a Friday evening? He opened his mouth to say something and she knew exactly what it would be. About timing and wanting to get things done in a hurry.

"Come over, to eat," she suggested, making a bold offer.

"Come over?"

"Ginny is usually out with her friend and ... and ..." She swallowed her embarrassment, conscious of the fact that she still hadn't determined if he was single or not. He didn't wear a ring, but it was possible that he might have a girlfriend now, given that many years had passed since the tragedy of his other girlfriend.

She hadn't plucked up the courage to swing the conversation around to that topic and get a firm answer from him. It was important to know because she looked forward to seeing him each day, and the idea of having such an intense reaction to a man who might not be available sat uneasy with her.

His expression sobered. "And you don't like eating alone?"

She loved when he completed her sentences, when he could sense she was struggling to make her point. "I hate eating alone. I... I like coming here because ... "

"You don't want to be home alone."

"Yes." She didn't want to be home alone and he was an easy distraction from her worries.

He reached back, placing his hand on his shoulder blade, giving her another view of his flexed bicep.

Oh my.

"I mean, if it's okay with you, I'd love to come over," he said. Their eyes held and met.

"Great." She turned around, taking off her overalls, and letting out a breath she didn't know she'd been holding.

"I'll take my truck," he offered, probably noting that she

hadn't driven over this time. The short ride would be enough time for her to gather her feelings, to compose herself and to wonder what on earth she was going to cook that would be easy and quick.

CHAPTER 18

"*I* love you, Gin."

Ben ran his hand over her belly and kissed it, making her giggle. The baby kicked. She'd started feeling these flutters only recently and it made everything so real. This baby was real, a new life was moving inside her, and it wouldn't be long before she became a mother.

"He kicked!" Ben looked up at her. He was sitting on a chair in the kitchen, and she was standing between his legs.

Things were good again between them. Not long after she had canceled the wedding, he'd called her a few times to see how she was. At first she'd ignored him, his infidelity prickling like a thorn in her heart.

She'd told Talia, and her friend had advised her that Ben was moping around town looking lost, but to not give him an inch.

Then Ginny had told Talia her baby secret, and sworn her to secrecy. Her friend had highlighted the problems of being a single mom, and she'd given Ginny some things to think about that Ginny herself hadn't yet considered. "You'll meet someone," Talia told her. "It will happen."

But then she'd run into Ben at the supermarket. He'd looked at her as if he'd seen a ghost. Guilt mixed with sadness on the face she had come to know so well and love so much. "How are you doing, Gin?"

And from there she'd started seeing him, had listened to his explanations of how sorry he was that he'd ruined things between them, how he'd never done anything like that before, and how he'd been so drunk, how his friends had plied him with so much drink he couldn't think clearly. "Nothing happened, babe." And a part of her wanted to believe him. Had needed to believe him, for the sake of their unborn child. She had to trust him. The baby needed a father, and wouldn't it be better for her to have faith if Ben was remorseful and willing to try again?

Just like that, she had agreed when he suggested that they get back together again, that they give things another try, for the sake of the baby. He seemed genuinely sorry, and looked so rough, as if he hadn't slept, as if his whole world had imploded.

It had happened a few weeks after Ashleigh had gone, and she couldn't handle the constant bickering between her and Eloise.

Eloise was better in small doses, whereas Ashleigh was a wonderful diplomat. Ginny missed her oldest sister, but when Ashleigh asked to extend her trip, Ginny's spirit hit rock bottom. She was tired and the morning sickness made everything twenty times worse.

When she told Ben about the baby, he was so happy, he started to cry. He was a changed man. He was remorseful and he was worth giving another chance to. Keeping their romance a secret from Eloise and Talia, hadn't been easy. She'd lied to her sister and gone out with Ben when she'd told Eloise it was Talia she was seeing.

Slowly, over time, she fell back in love with him. She still loved him. The weeks spent with him, getting to re-ignite what they'd had, made her life better, especially when there was only home and Eloise to go back to.

She later told Talia but her friend didn't approve and said she was making a mistake, so Ginny stopped telling her. Stopped seeing her.

She and Ben were back to how they used to be before that terrible weekend of their breakup. He was so besotted with her, with the pregnancy, and the idea of becoming a father, and not a day passed when he didn't tell Ginny how much he loved her and how much he regretted what had happened.

She believed him because he was the father and she wanted him back in her life. She didn't want to be a single mother. She couldn't see how another man would be interested in her when she had given birth to another man's child.

It had to be Ben. Her baby needed him as much as she did.

But she was risking things, telling Eloise. Letting her see that she and Ben were back together. Going home with him tonight—it could go either way.

She'd lain awake at night wondering how to tell her sister. It would have been much easier to tell Ashleigh. Ash would have understood. She might have been annoyed initially, but she would have eventually understood.

The baby kicked again, and Ben looked up at her, his eyes sparkling with love. That's what he felt for the baby, she could see it as clear as day. She needed him to be on her side. Eloise hadn't taken the news of her pregnancy too well, and even though she was doing her best to put on a brave face, Ginny sensed an underlying tension between them.

Not having Talia as an ally, and with Ash out of the country, she only had Ben. The baby kicked again and she giggled as Ben's hand slipped under her baggy blouse and swept over her blossoming belly. His touch was electric; it was the first time he'd touched her there, under the fabric.

"See, babe." He stared up at her. "You feel it too?" The baby kicked again. "She's so active!"

"She?"

"I want a little girl. I want her to be just like you." Her heart melted. He stood and wrapped his arms around her, making her feel cherished. "I'm going to keep you safe, babe. I'm going to help you raise our baby."

Her insides turned all gooey and warm. "That's what I want as well, a baby girl." She also didn't want to be here, living with her sisters, bringing up a child in the same house where she'd grown up. She wanted her own place. She and Ben hadn't decided what to do about the house they'd bought together; the house they'd lovingly furnished together. Her life had been like a rollercoaster ride for so long now, and she hadn't had the time or energy to decide what to do with it, but things worked out, didn't they? That house was ready and waiting for them to move back into. A home for their family.

That's where the baby belonged. In a home with its mother and father. She had forgiven Ben, surely her sisters would, too?

"I love you, Gin. I love you and the baby, and I love that you've given me a second chance." He pressed his lips to hers and she fell into another one of his delicious kisses. She'd missed being held, and hugged, and kissed.

Being loved and having a sense of belonging.

His kiss deepened, turned hot and urgent. She hadn't done more than this, taking small baby steps, but Ben had needs and she could sense his growing desire for her.

"I want to take it slow," she moaned, as his hand slid around her waist then lowered.

"Sure, babe. Sure." He kissed her again, hot and needy. "I just want to kiss you. Nothing more. I've missed you so much."

She heard a loud gasp, and broke away from the embrace to find Eloise and the handyman staring at them. Eloise had turned as white as snow. Ben turned around slowly, this hand sliding away from her waist before holding her hand. Ginny's insides turned hollow. This wasn't how she'd wanted her sister to find out. Not with her and Ben kissing and his arms around her. She had planned to keep things respectful, but now it was too late.

"I should go," said Ben, his voice raspy as he gripped her hand firmly.

Eloise scoffed. Or maybe it was a little laugh. "You lied." Her voice was a snarl.

"I wanted to tell you." Ginny tried to free her hand from Ben's.

Even she wasn't that cruel.

"*This* is how you wanted to tell me?" Eloise's voice was so deathly quiet that it scared Ginny. She tried to free her hand from Ben, wanting to get closer to Eloise, to explain, to make things better. To let her know that she was okay. That it was good and right for her and Ben to get back together. But Ben didn't let go of her hand. She turned to him as she tried to wrench it away.

"Together forever, babe," he mouthed.

"Let go of my hand," Ginny demanded, shocked by his reaction, by his inability to read the situation.

"How could you?" Eloise cried, but she was staring at Ben, not Ginny.

"I love her," Ben protested. "Ginny told me. We're going to have a baby, and it's mine."

Ginny chewed her lip, hating that things had turned out so badly. She glanced at the handyman who still hovered around Eloise. He was staring at the floor, as he ran his hand over his neck as if he didn't know what to do.

"You love her?" Eloise cried, her face twisting. "You cheated on her!"

"I told her what happened." Ben's voice was eerily calm.

"You told her *your* version of it," Eloise snapped.

Ginny's arms hung at her sides slack. She felt a heaviness in her chest. She'd told Ben that this wasn't the way to do it; that him sitting in their home unexpectedly didn't seem right.

But he'd forced her, anyway.

She'd had all week to tell Eloise and she hadn't been able to. In the end, he'd suggested that they might as well put on a unified front. That the news would be a shock to Eloise, so why not shock her all at once and get it over with? She needed to see them together.

But. Not. Like. This.

"I'm sorry. I didn't want you to find out like this," Ginny whimpered, seeing that Eloise was still in shock, her face impassive, her eyes glazed over.

"You didn't'?" Eloise snarled. "Then what is this?" She jabbed a finger at them.

I've been trying to tell you all week."

"You've barely been here."

"That's not true. I made dinner the other night and I was trying to tell you but you're so judgemental. You've already made up your mind about Ben and nothing I say is going to shift your opinion of him."

"I want the best for you!" Eloise cried.

"What are you saying?" Ben growled. "How do you know what's best for her?"

"Because I'm her sister and I take care of her."

"You're not her favorite sister. All you do is argue with her and make her feel bad. Is that how you should be treating her in this condition?"

Ginny walked towards Eloise, wanting to make things

better, not worse. "I'm sorry you found out like this. I didn't want to shock you."

"It wasn't a complete shock. I've seen you both together."

Ginny gasped. "When? Where? And why didn't you say something?"

"Because I wanted to see how long you'd continue lying to me."

"I wanted to tell you!" Ginny wailed. "You're not an easy person to open up to."

"I've tried to be. I'm doing my best," Eloise threw back. She waved a hand in their direction. "How long has this been going on?"

"I should go," the handyman said again, and Ginny wished he would go. Eloise seemed to have forgotten that he was there. Her sister was still having problems accepting that she and Ben were a couple again. When the man touched Eloise's arm, his fingers trailing a few inches down, Ginny flinched in surprise. The touch seemed affectionate.

Was it possible that Eloise was up to something?

Eloise nodded. "I can stay if you want," he told her.

"I'll be okay. Sorry about this."

Sorry about this? Ginny craned her neck forward, examining the body language between her sister and the handyman.

Sorry for what?

Did Eloise have plans with this new man of hers? Ginny could have sworn her sister had another man over in Hyannis Port, someone she'd been keen to meet in Miami.

There was more to this than met the eye. And to think that Eloise had the audacity to be angry with her? Ginny couldn't believe that her sister was annoyed at her for getting back with her ex. At least she had something with Ben. Their baby bound her and Ben together.

He had barely left the room when Ginny couldn't resist. "Did we ruin your plans for the evening?"

Eloise lifted one shoulder in a shrug. "There were no plans. But it seems like I messed up yours."

Her sister walked out and in the next moment, Ginny heard her footsteps thudding loudly as she ran up the stairs.

"I wanted you to know!" she shouted. Ben came up behind her and put his hands on her shoulders. "Don't look so worried, babe. At least she knows now."

CHAPTER 19

*E*loise ran up the stairs, needing to get away from Ben and Ginny. The image of them kissing had burned a hole right through her.

She flung her phone onto the bed and overcome with nausea, ran into the bathroom and knelt over the basin. She heaved, but nothing came out. Then she pulled down the toilet seat and sat on it.

She hadn't heard Ginny's footsteps. Her sister probably didn't care about Eloise's opinion. The fact remained: Ginny and Ben were definitely together.

Not only did Ben know of Ginny's pregnancy, but Liam did, too, and if he knew, there was a danger that Ford could find out, as well as Darcie. Rumors would spread faster than a fire, and she couldn't let the townspeople know before Ashleigh did.

What to do? That was the question. It felt as if Ginny and Ben were on one side and she on the other.

She washed her hands, then threw some cold water over her face as thoughts flew around in her head.

She'd have to face Ben and Ginny, and acting calm and collected was the way to go.

Not this, rushing upstairs to get away. She would have to do better.

Be better.

Be like Ashleigh.

As she walked out, she heard her phone vibrating on her bed, and she rushed to get it.

"Yes." She felt weary, deflated, resigned.

"You okay?" Liam's voice reverberated inside her chest.

"I was going to call you," she said, lying on the bed, a small burst of happiness fighting through the dull ache.

"I've been calling you."

"You have?" She stared at her phone and saw she had three missed calls.

"I was worried about you. I wanted to see if you were okay."

She could listen to that rich, deep voice all day and night. "Oh. I'm okay."

"I don't expect you to be okay, but I wanted to check in on you."

"That's ... that's kind of you." She allowed herself to exhale properly. Up until then she'd been holding it all in, shallow breaths, muscles tight, tension all over her body.

"I was waiting outside. Your sister has suspicions and I didn't want to give her more ammunition."

She laughed. "Don't worry about Ginny. She's being silly. Also, you didn't have to wait for me, but I appreciate it all the same."

"Like I said, I wanted to make sure you were okay."

"You don't have to worry about me. I'm a tough cookie. Ginny shocked me, she really did, but I'll get over it."

"I know that. I can see it. But it seems like your entire world fell apart. I know it must have been a shock for you to see your sister with... that guy."

"Did Ford tell you about him?" she asked, knowing that she had kept everything about Ginny in the dark.

"A little."

"I wasn't expecting that. I saw her that day you roped me into getting the paint. I saw them in the parking lot."

"I saw them, too. I figured," Liam told her.

"I prayed that they were only talking. That it was nothing more than that."

She waited for Liam to say something, but he was silent, and she suddenly longed to see his face again. She got up and looked out of the window, but the summer house was in the distance, its back was to her. She pressed a hand to her chest, while clasping the cell phone to her ear. Closing her eyes, it was easy to imagine that he was here beside her.

She needed that. Longed for it. Some closeness and intimacy, with a man she could trust. But that was the hard part, finding a man she could trust. "Now you know the little secret we've been trying to keep hidden?" she asked, needing him to promise that it would remain a secret. Ashleigh would be so angry if she were the last to find out.

"I do."

"I'd appreciate it if you didn't say a word to anyone."

"Say no more. I saw nothing, and I'm sorry that you were so shook up. I feel like your sister is vulnerable and maybe not in a good place, but I feel she maybe could have handled that better."

"Please don't tell Ford."

"Don't you trust me?"

"I—" She heard a knock on her door and as she glanced in that direction, Ginny walked in, her face hard.

"Ben left." Then her gaze went to the cell phone. "I didn't know you were on the phone. Who are you talking to, the handyman or Alex?"

Eloise froze. This was the worst possible moment for Ginny to come in. Her sister made no attempt to whisper, and Liam had probably heard her. "I have to go. I'm sorry," she told him, and quickly hung up. She turned to Ginny. "You did that on purpose."

"I did not!" Ginny cried, looking genuinely surprised. "Was that him? The handyman?"

"His name is Liam."

"Exactly how *handy* did he get with you?"

Heat raced through Eloise's body and she jumped to standing. "Did you come in here to start another argument?"

"I wanted to explain everything to you but there seems to be double standards in play."

"Double standards?" Eloise shrieked, feeling confused. "What double standards?"

"You met someone when you went to the wedding, and you've been trying to sneak off to go and see him."

"Is that a crime?"

"No, but why keep it a secret?" Ginny challenged. "Ash and I didn't truly believe that you were sick that time."

"I was sick!"

"I'm pretty sure you just wanted to have more time with your secret lover."

"I don't have a secret lover."

"You don't have to lie about it. I don't care who you've met, but I don't appreciate you lying to us about wanting to have a longer vacation!"

"I'm not with anyone, and I don't have a secret *lover.*" She was about to fold her arms when she stopped, knowing that it would make her seem defensive. Maybe it was time to come clean, to be honest? "I met someone. Alex, and I was attracted to him. We had fun, laughing and joking and getting along. It was nice, but nothing serious happened." She swallowed, thinking back to the wedding. It had been fun with flirtation. Nothing heavy or serious.

"But you were hoping something would have happened?" Ginny asked, her voice turning soft for the first time in a long time.

Eloise shrugged. "I'm not so sure now. I canceled the trip to Miami because you were sick."

"Don't blame me for that."

"I'm not blaming you," she countered.

"And so you're hoping to strike up something with this guy?"

"Liam, and no nothing has been *struck* up." Eloise nostrils flared with anger. The audacity of Ginny. Making out in the kitchen, shocking the living daylights out of Eloise and now her sister was making this be about Eloise and Liam.

Nothing was going on.

Nothing real, or physical.

A flurry of emotions whirled inside Eloise's mind. There were feelings going on, but Ginny wasn't an empath. To the contrary, her sister was spoiled and self-obsessed, so if she'd noticed something, maybe the attraction was strong enough that others could see it, too?

After all, Liam had called her. He'd wanted to know that she was okay. That had to count for something. "What happened tonight isn't about me, Gin. It's about you." And, just like that, the wind went out of her and she collapsed in a heap on the bed.

"Look. I don't want to fight with you. You're my sister. I love you." She held out her hand, her body turning soft as the anger went out of it. "I don't want you to be hurt, and right now, you're more vulnerable than ever. I wish you'd told me that you and Ben were together. I'd seen the two of you together, but seeing you two together in the kitchen, hugging and kissing, that was a shock I hadn't been expecting."

"You saw us before"

"In the parking lot. Liam and I went to the home improvement center and I saw you both."

"Why didn't you say anything?"

Eloise let out a sigh. "I was waiting for you to say something first. I tried to get you to tell me, I tried to give you a chance but you lied."

"Because I didn't know how you'd take it," Ginny cried. "I was scared you'd be angry with me, which was the reason why I didn't tell you about the baby."

Eloise chewed her lip. She could have handled that better. The pregnancy news was a shock, but this, Ginny getting back with Ben, that was hard to take. "I don't want him to hurt you again."

"He won't." Ginny insisted. She sounded so certain, but Eloise knew. She'd been bitten once and she would never have gone back to her ex.

"How can you be so sure?" she asked Ginny. "He did it once, and right before your wedding. Who does that?"

Ginny flung her arms up in a gesture of annoyance. "There you go again, being all nasty and not giving him the benefit of the doubt."

"It's the truth, Gin. I want you to see the truth, and if Ash were here she'd want the same. I want you to go into this with open eyes."

"He's the father of my child. He feels bad and sad, and he's misunderstood."

Eloise swallowed and fisted her hands together in an effort not to roll her eyes.

Misunderstood?

"He feels bad for what happened, and he says he loves me.

He says nothing happened with that other woman that night, and he's been feeling lost and lonely without me and…"

Eloise scoffed in disbelief. "If he was feeling so lost and lonely why didn't he come looking for you sooner?"

"Because he didn't know how I'd react. He didn't know how you and Ash would react. We ran into one another one day. It was soon after Ash left, and I was glad for the extra company. Things at home weren't so great. You were moody and miserable."

Eloise ground her teeth together, trying not to protest. Trying to listen silently.

"He said he missed me, said I looked good, and he'd been worried about me and had wanted to reach out but wasn't sure how to. He was sweet. We started calling and texting more, and … I was happy to get out of the house and talk to someone who understood me."

"It was because of me?" Eloise gasped. If Ash had been here, this would not have happened. Not only did she feel like a failure, but if she was the reason Ginny had gone running to Ben, then she would never forgive herself.

"Talia doesn't approve."

This was news to Eloise's ears. "She knows? About the baby?"

"I've sworn her to secrecy. We can't have other people finding out before Ash does, but I had to tell her after Ben and I got back together and she wasn't happy. And you weren't easy to be around, either, so I only had Ben."

"I'm sorry I was so difficult to be around." She'd been exactly how Ginny had described and if she could go back and change it all, she would. If it meant that Ben wouldn't be with Ginny, she'd do it.

There was a chance maybe that they could work out.

Ashleigh would be the optimistic one who'd hope, for

Ginny and the baby's sake that it would, but Eloise saw no future.

There was never a future with a man who cheated.

"I can't bring up this baby alone."

Seeing the sadness in Ginny's eyes made Eloise throw a comforting arm around her sister's shoulder. "You will never be alone."

"A baby needs a father."

"A baby needs a *good* father." She tried to soften the blow. "People can change," she said slowly, knowing that this wasn't something she believed. Once bitten, she would never give anyone a chance. "But can you trust him, Gin?" Ginny was different. Naive, hopeful. Maybe life would be okay for her.

Ginny looked at her hopelessly, then shrugged. Eloise tried to channel Ashleigh, and how she would handle this. "People can change, I guess. You'll always have your family. We'll always have your back, Gin. You're the baby of our family and you will always be looked after." She half-smiled.

"I'm not the baby anymore." Ginny leaned closer towards Eloise. "There's going to be a new baby in the family."

They hugged tightly, then, and after their embrace, Eloise kept her arm around Ginny's shoulder and kept her close. "I love you Ginny. I'm sorry I couldn't deal with this the way Ash would have. I'm sorry I can't be more like Ash."

"I shouldn't be so hard on you. It's not easy for you either. I know I've been a brat, but I didn't mean to lie to you. The only reason I hid the truth from you was because you didn't handle the pregnancy news well, and I was wary about mentioning this. You're so vocal about Ben; you and Ash hate him so much."

"After what he did to you, yes, but …" She paused, seeing Ginny's mood turn somber. "But if you believe him, and you have faith in him, who am I to judge?" She stared down at her hand. "You're right. Your baby needs a father."

"I lie awake at night because I worry about what sort of mother I'll be, and whether my baby will have enough—"

"Your baby will always have enough. You don't need to worry about money, or security or anything. We have a business, and its successful, and ..." Eloise stopped talking. She'd had plans to leave the town and move on, but lately those plans had fallen by the wayside but, according to Ford, Ash wanted more time on her trip. Eloise was beginning to wonder if her sister had plans to ever come back.

Someone had to stay here in Whisper Falls to take care of Ginny and the baby if things with Ben didn't work out. "You'll always have family around you, Gin. Stop worrying. You'll never have to worry about your future or your baby's future."

"But there's nothing like having two parents, right? Look at us, look how we suffered, even though Ash and Aunty Becky did their best to raise us and they did well, but we ... we've lost out, haven't we?" Her sister's voice trailed to a sad whisper. "I want my baby to know that I did my best in giving his or her dad a second chance."

"I hear you, Gin. I hear you." She lifted Ginny's hand and pressed a kiss on it.

"I can't be in your hair forever. Ash is loving her newfound freedom, and when she comes back, she and Ford might get married." Ginny poked her gently with her elbow. "You might get married again. I saw the way the handyman—"

"His name is Liam."

"You're sounding uptight. *Liam*, then. I saw the way he looked at you."

"How was he looking at me?"

Ginny's eyes flashed with mischief. "Stop pretending nothing's going on."

"Nothing *is* going on."

"I saw the way he touched you."

Heat warmed Eloise's cheeks. "He didn't touch me."

"To get your attention when he was leaving, he did. He likes you. He likes you a lot. Stop pretending and tell me what's going on in that summer house of yours, because you've been spending a lot of time there."

Eloise stood up. "I've been helping him paint."

Ginny raised an eyebrow, suspicion spreading like a rash all over her face. "Helping him paint? Is that what they call it these days?" She broke out into a fit of laughter. Eloise watched her, and felt at peace. It had been a long time since she'd heard that sound from Ginny.

Contentment swept over her. Things were looking up. Maybe there was a place for Ben in Ginny's life with the new baby. Maybe he could redeem himself. "You need to get to bed. Have you eaten?" She hadn't had dinner, and poor Liam had gone home hungry.

"I haven't had dinner. Believe it or not we were waiting for you to come home."

"Believe it or not, this was the first time I asked Liam to come over and eat."

"Because you like him."

"Because I didn't think you'd be at home," said Eloise, grinning.

"And because you like him."

CHAPTER 20

*E*loise had no intention of telling Ashleigh, but she desperately needed her older sister to sound off on.

She missed Ashleigh. She missed the late-night conversations when they'd all sit around the table after dinner. Funny how she'd felt hemmed in by it all, and now that it was gone, she missed the warm familiarity and comfort of her sisters.

She also didn't know how to deal with it all. There was so much going on, she felt guilty and anxious about keeping it from her sister. Only one thing kept her grounded and sane in all the mess, and that was Liam. She kept him in the background of her thoughts, like a warm, comfortable blanket, something she could reach out and grab for when life turned hard.

But now she felt happier for making up with Ginny; it was always better to get on and have a happy home, than letting the tension consume their moods and personalities.

"Turn your camera on," Ashleigh ordered.

"Why?"

"So I can see you, silly."

It was early morning there, which meant it would be after midday where Ashleigh was. Somewhere in Italy.

Eloise tried to hold out, but she failed.

"Your camera!" Ashleigh said.

Eloise's sucked in a breath. She didn't want to turn her camera on. Ashleigh had a laser vision which could easily penetrate across the screen and she'd soon discover that something was wrong. No matter how positively she tried to think about Ben, Eloise couldn't shake the heavy feeling that Ginny was making a mistake.

People didn't change.

A man like Ben couldn't. If he'd been a good man, he would never have done the things he'd done to hurt Ginny.

Eloise didn't blame Ginny for her blind naivete in looking for the good in him; her sister was desperate and not thinking straight. She'd suffered two life-changing events—a wedding which didn't go through, and then discovering she was pregnant.

Well, going forward, she was going to fix everything. She was going to be there for Ginny, even if it meant keeping her lips locked every time Ben was around.

She pretended to fiddle with it. "I can't turn it on."

"What?"

She didn't want to lie to Ashleigh even more than she was already. "Oh, there you go." She reluctantly turned her camera on.

A smiling, golden, blossoming Ashleigh stared at her before bolting forward. "What's wrong?"

Eloise forced her lips into another smile. "Nothing. You worry too much."

"We didn't have a group call planned for today, and the fact that you're calling me now makes me worry that something is up. And why are you calling me so early?" Ashleigh's eyes narrowed with suspicion.

"Because I didn't want to call you when I got back from work. You're four or five hours ahead of me."

Ash inclined her head, as if she was processing this news and didn't yet know whether to believe her or not. "We usually have our video calls on Sunday. Also, where's Ginny?"

Eloise forced a laugh, then kept her smile plastered on her face. "Look at you, worrying for no reason. There's nothing wrong. I missed you and I wanted to call, and I didn't want to have to wait until Sunday. Unless ... you're busy."

"I was doing some yoga, if you must ask." Ashleigh turned her cell phone to show a yoga mat on the floor, and then to show that she was in her workout clothes. "I miss the back yard. It's nice to do this in the back yard with the sun on you."

An awkward pause ballooned between them.

"You'll be back soon," Eloise said brightly, before waiting for Ashleigh's reaction. Ford already knew about it, and she'd been wondering when her sister would tell her.

Eloise stared at her and Ashleigh stared right back. "You're acting strange."

Eloise forced another laugh. "I'm not! You are."

"I was planning to go to Turkey. I mean, it's not important. I don't have to go now I can always go another time..."

"Another time?" The words sent a shiver down Eloise's spine. Ashleigh had caught the travel bug and was making plans.

To go again. Another time. Which meant she would make this a yearly thing.

Which meant that Eloise would be forever holding the fort.

And with Ginny's baby, Eloise would be working and babysitting and taking care of the family.

Liam would be long gone.

"Unless you and Ginny need me back ..."

Of course they needed her back. They needed her back a month ago.

"Turkey, huh?" Eloise picked off an imaginary thread from her jeans. "It sounds rather exotic."

"Oh, it is. According to what I've heard."

"There's so much of the world to see," Ashleigh gushed. She was always so passionate when she talked about the places she'd been to and the places she dreamed of going to.

"There is," Eloise mused, while wondering how much damage would be done to her sister's mood and subsequently her trip, if Eloise allowed the words on the tip of her tongue to fall.

Ginny is pregnant, and she's back with Ben.

"Ford would have loved this," Ashleigh continued, her voice turning softer.

Now was her chance to ask that million-dollar question. "Why didn't you ask him to go with you?"

"Maybe I should have."

"It's not too late," Eloise offered.

"It's not." Ashleigh ran a hand through her now golden mane. She didn't have a care or a worry in the world. Here she was, rambling about her travels and looking relaxed and beautiful.

It wasn't fair.

Eloise could feel her heart pounding in her chest. The weight of the news, the real weight, not the airy-fairy nice words she'd said to Ginny yesterday, was like a boulder on her chest.

The hard reality of Ginny's situation was that if Ben messed up again, he'd break Ginny's heart forever and an innocent child would be involved.

She had to tell Ash. She had to. "I...wanted to... to... to say..." But her mouth turned dry.

Ashleigh flapped her hand across her face, as if she were too hot, or worried. Or irritated. "What is it? Say it."

It all flashed by like a montage in a sad movie, all the bad things that could go wrong. And everyone would know that she was weak, that she'd ruined her sister's vacation by telling her.

So, she decided not to.

"You seem to be having an awesome time out there. You look amazing and it's the most relaxed we've seen you, so, if you want to stay for a little longer, why don't you?"

Ashleigh's face lit up like a ray of sunshine. "You mean it?"

"I do. We're fine here. Perfectly fine. We have a great system going and you coming back would mess it all up."

Ashleigh laughed, placing a hand on her chest. Her fingers looked so elegant; she'd painted them a rose blush pink, and she wore her hair slightly differently, too, to one side and with it catching the sun, it looked nothing like the dirty blonde of before. Sunkissed golden streaks brought out the hazel in her eyes more. Ashleigh looked younger, happier. She was effervescent, and Eloise had no right to take that away from her.

"Are you sure?" Ashleigh asked.

"Ask me that again and I'll order you to come back."

"Thanks. I was going to ask you; I was plucking up the courage to say it."

Another sister plucking up the courage to talk to her? Eloise felt ashamed. "You too? You think I'm a dragon as well?"

Ashleigh's eyes popped wide open with surprise. "Did Ginny say you were a dragon?"

"Not in those words."

"Is she okay now? Is she over him?"

Eloise could feel her eyebrows lifting slightly. "Don't talk to me about him. Ginny's fine. She's absolutely fine."

Ashleigh let out a sigh. "Thank you. I won't delay my trip again. I promise. It's just that I left it so late to do this and I want to see everything, but I'm still young enough to come back." There was a tone of regret in her voice.

"Why so sad?" Eloise noticed the sudden change in her sister's demeanor as different as night and day.

"I met a wonderful elderly couple in Rome and we got talking. They were going to visit the Amalfi coast where they went on their honeymoon, and now that they were both retired, they were visiting again. They were doing a two-week visit, and the elderly woman said that this time they had to make sure they saw everything because there would be no coming back. This would be their last chance. They were in their eighties."

Eloise felt a pinch of sadness on hearing that. "That's profound."

"Yes."

She swallowed. "You're not even fifty yet, Ash."

"I know. I know."

"You still have plenty of time to see the world."

"I wasn't thinking of me." Her voice faded to a whisper. "I was thinking of mom and dad. They died so young. It was so cruel how their lives were cut so… so…"

Eloise strained to hear as Ashleigh's voice tapered to a whisper, but she knew what her sister meant to say.

Short.

Their lives had been cut so short.

Eloise swallowed, forcing the sob that was stuck in her throat to stay there. Ashleigh dabbed at her eyes, then asked, "So, what's the new system?"

"What new system?"

"The one you said you'd put in place at the shop."

"Oh that ..." She playfully swatted the air, while scrambling to think of something to say. "It's easy. I go in on Saturday, and Ginny makes dinner."

"Ginny makes dinner every night?"

Another white lie. "Yes."

CHAPTER 21

It hadn't stopped gnawing at him like a gnat.

Once again Ford had seen Ben with Ginny, this time in the diner, eating together. Holding hands and acting like they were back together again.

Problem was, he'd seen Ben not too long ago, with another woman, in a bar out of town. They weren't wrapped around one another, but it had been just the two of them and Ford would have forgotten all about it, but seeing him with Ginny again hit Ford in the gut like a punch. He'd seen her in the aftermath, after the wedding had been called off, and he'd known the reason behind it. He'd seen how she'd fallen apart and he knew first-hand how worried her sisters had been.

He needed peace of mind. He needed to know that Ginny would never get back with that rascal and they were nothing more than friends. It was this assurance that he sought which made him walk into the bridal shop at closing time. This was the best way to avoid the customers and the other shop assistants and get Eloise by herself.

Catching sight of her hunched over her diary, he strode

towards her slowly, a nervous feeling welling up in his stomach. "Hey."

She looked up and moved the diary to one side. She looked tired, he noted. He nodded. "You okay?"

"Just tired, and glad it's the end of the day."

"You're not staying late?"

"I haven't been, lately."

"That's good to hear." He nodded again, prompting her, because it seemed as if she was about to say something. When she remained silent, he coughed lightly. "So, how are things?"

"They're rolling along."

That was a non-committal answer if ever he heard one. "All good?"

She paused, eyeing him carefully. "All good. What are you doing, Ford? Are you checking up on me?"

"What? Me? No." His voice dipped a little, the insistence wavering.

"Because I've never seen you come here as often as you have been ever since my sister left."

"That's because I want to see if I can get any more news about Ashleigh from you."

"Are you still trying to pretend that you don't talk to my sister while she's a whole other continent away?"

"'Course I do. We talk a lot, if you must know. I want to hear about her from you as well."

"We spoke this morning."

"You did?" His voice perked up and he waited in anticipation. If he had his way he'd call Ashleigh every day, but he sensed she was busy, that she had things to do and places to see, and as hard as it was to put a finger on it, he was beginning to feel as if he was in the way—even given the fact that he was all the way across the Atlantic, and he missed her. Something seemed off to him, and he only called once a week, and left it to her to contact him if she needed to.

Eloise nodded. "I don't know where to start." The color slowly drained from her face and it looked as if she was about to say something. Come to think about it, Eloise looked as if she hadn't slept well last night.

"About what?" He needed information from her, but she looked as if she needed some comforting herself.

"Oh." She scratched her neck, turning all anxious and fidgety. Something Eloise never was.

"Is Ashleigh okay?" It was his biggest worry, her being all the way in another country, without a friend or family close by. She'd never left Whisper Falls, and while he understood her desire to travel, it scared him a little because he loved her and wanted her to be safe.

"She was sad. She told me about wanting to stay a bit longer. I didn't tell her that you'd already told me, and I could have done with her being back but ... she was sad."

"Sad, why?" His gut clenched and he could feel this wasn't going to end well. If Ashleigh was in trouble, he'd be on the next plane to go and make sure she was okay.

"She was remembering our parents, about how they died so young, and ..." She looked away and sniffled, as if trying to hold back tears

He moved towards her, wanting to comfort her. "Hey, hey. What happened is a tragedy, and the loss for your family has been huge. Irreplaceable. It was cruel to have lost your parents when they were so young, when you all were so young." His voice cracked. It broke him just to think about that time.

But at that very moment Eloise crumbled in front of his eyes. She let out a gasp then burst out crying.

They weren't silent tears.

She was sobbing.

Loud, heart-breaking sobs, as if she'd been holding it all in and could no longer.

He was at her side in an instant, putting one big arm awkwardly around her shoulder. He didn't know how to comfort her without invading her personal space.

She wasn't Ashleigh. He'd have blanketed her and hugged her to his chest. He'd have held her until the sobs subsided.

But this was Eloise, and she was strong. She could weather anything. For as long as he'd known her she'd been a tough cookie. Resilient. She always put on a strong face. She was spiky and hard edged, and this was the first time he'd seen beneath the exterior.

He rubbed his brow with his free hand, feeling helpless, hearing Eloise sob. "I'm sorry. I shouldn't have said anything. I didn't mean to bring it all back."

She took a deep breath, and he, eyeing a box of tissues nearby, moved away to grab it. He pulled a few out and handed them to her.

"Sorry," she said, wiping her face then blowing her nose. She whipped up a new tissue then wiped her face again and dabbed the corners of her eyes.

He waited patiently.

"Ginny's pregnant."

"Pregnant?" He was sure he'd misheard.

"Pregnant and carrying Ben's child."

His heart dipped inside his ribcage. "They're together? It's true?"

She looked up at him expectantly. "You knew?"

He had to tell her, but he didn't have to tell her everything. He prayed that the boy had sense and wasn't cheating on Ginny. The scoundrel seemed to bounce from woman to woman, but now a baby was involved. He prayed that Ben had changed.

Eloise's eyes blazed as she glared at him. "Did Liam tell you?"

Liam already knew? "Tell me what?" he asked slowly. Eloise was often quick to point fingers. What Liam had to do with all of this, he didn't know.

"I saw them together. Ginny and Ben, in town one day, and Liam saw them too, and I told him not to say anything to you because I knew it would upset you. I didn't think they were together then, but I saw them again earlier today, at the diner and they looked very happy together. Very much *together*."

"That's because they are together."

"And the baby?" He was confused. "How did that come about?"

Eloise lowered her head and sighed. "A momentary lapse of judgement and being reckless, so Ginny says. Happened just before they broke up."

"And the baby is due when?"

"In the new year. She's four and a half months pregnant."

He swiped his hand over his jaw, assimilating the news, trying to make sense of it, trying to figure out what it meant for all of them. "Halfway through."

"Don't remind me. Every day I wake up wondering what I should do," Eloise wailed. "What do I do? It's been so hard keeping it all to myself. I've been wanting to tell Ashleigh but I didn't, knowing that if I did she'd come rushing home."

"She doesn't know?" The news smacked him dead center in his stomach.

"About the pregnancy?" Eloise bit her lip. "No, she doesn't know, and she also doesn't know that Ginny's back with Ben."

"Who knows?"

"You, me, Ben, Talia, Ginny's friend, and Liam."

"Most people except for Ashleigh." The fact that Liam already knew confirmed his suspicions. That man always seemed to have a question or two about Eloise, but Ford had seen right through him. And, it wasn't a bad thing. Not a bad thing at all.

"I didn't know about any of this until after she'd left. Learning about the pregnancy was a big shock, and now finding out that Ginny's back with Ben, I'm at my wits end. Ashleigh will hate me for not telling her, but she also can't do anything about it and I know she's on the trip of a lifetime, so I haven't yet told her. But is that the right thing to do? You tell me?"

He swiped both hands across his cheeks, knowing how protective Ashleigh was about her family, and how this was the most life-changing news that could happen, and for Ashleigh to be thousands of miles away and ignorant, was not good.

But he felt a sense of responsibility now that Eloise had confided in him and knowing that she had no one, apart from Liam it seemed like, he was glad to be of some help. "For now," he said, thinking it was the right move for now because there was nothing Ashleigh could do if she knew. She'd only worry about it, and she looked so relaxed, so beautiful, so happy. She deserved this vacation and he didn't want anything to ruin her trip. Her travel plans, and other dreams, had been broken years ago. It wasn't fair to do that to her again.

But there would be hell to pay when she returned. He'd have to figure out a way to handle that. "She'll be home soon," he said, hoping to reassure Eloise.

"She told me about Turkey," Eloise commented.

"Good. About time, too. How do you feel about her staying on a little longer?" He finally understood why Eloise seemed so tired lately. She was doing more than just standing in for the business and filling in for Ashleigh.

"I wish she hadn't, given what's happening here, but since she's over there, and there's not much she can do here, I'm okay with it. I'm not going to tell her."

"But can you handle things alone? She would have been coming back a month from now, but instead she's staying on an extra month."

The worry lines reappeared on Eloise's brow. "Ginny will be seven months pregnant by the time Ashleigh returns. That's too late."

"That's too long for her to go without knowing. While your sister deserves to have her vacation, what you've told me is worrying. It's life changing. Ashleigh would want to know." He put himself into Ashleigh's shoes. She would be livid.

"I told her she could stay for longer, because what can she do about it? Nothing. But I'm hoping there's a chance she'll get homesick and want to come home early."

"We can only hope. I'm here for whatever you decide."

Eloise put her arms around his waist and hugged him. "Thank you. Thank you." Then she pushed away quickly.

"You don't have to thank me. I'm glad to share your burden. It can't be easy for you to stand by and watch Ginny make her plans for the future while forgetting what happened."

"Then you agree with my worries about her getting back with Ben?"

He most certainly did. Eloise didn't know what he knew, and his worries were compounded.

"It's not me being paranoid?" she asked. "Ginny thinks I hate Ben because of what happened in my marriage."

It was only recently that he'd learned about the reason behind Eloise's divorce. Ashleigh had told him that Eloise's ex cheating on her had broken Eloise's trust, and behind that sunny demeanor, behind the party-girl façade, she was covering up rejection and betrayal. "It's not you being paranoid. You're not alone in this, okay? You can talk to me whenever it all gets to be too much. Anytime you need me, you pick up the phone and I'll be there. If you need to talk, or vent, or let it out, or if Ginny needs anything, you let me know."

"Thank you. I appreciate it." She rubbed a touch of lip balm along her lips. "I was so desperate to tell someone and I'm glad I could let it all out to you. I called Ashleigh because I couldn't sleep, and I needed to speak to someone. It helps that Ginny and I are now talking again."

"You weren't before?"

"We haven't been getting along too well, not since Ashleigh left. Ash is her favorite and she would have handled this so much better."

He tried to reassure her. "You're doing the best you can."

But now the itch that he'd been trying to ignore was back again. What if Ben still wasn't loyal to Ginny? Should he tell Eloise that he'd seen Ben with another woman not so long ago? Seeing her red eyes and tear-stained face, the answer deep in his chest was a resounding 'No.'

"I was so tempted to tell her this morning. I almost did, but then I stopped myself."

"Good."

"I stopped because she got all sad and teary remembering my mom and dad, and she'd met this couple ..." She told him all about the elderly couple who were trying to fit in their last bit of sightseeing.

"Why don't you surprise her?" Eloise cried, as if she'd had a lightbulb moment.

"Surprise her?" He frowned, although it had crossed his mind a couple of times to do that. To make a long-haul trip for a week or so, to maybe make up for the trip they'd planned to Europe a long time ago but had never taken.

Besides, he missed Ashleigh. He'd do anything to see her. The woman had decided to go away for more than four months, soon after they'd gotten back together.

"She said she misses you, and I think she would be really happy to see you."

But a part of him wasn't sure. Mindful of his divorce, and of what people might think, that he was needy and desperate to not be alone. Heck, even Ashleigh might think that.

"She will need to know at some point. Telling her over the phone isn't ideal, and if we wait until November when she returns, Ginny will be huge. The shock of seeing her will be too much, and then to tell her that Ginny is back with Ben, don't you see that it might be too much for her to take in all at once? I'm scared she might turn her back and run away as fast as she can."

"Your sister?" Ford scoffed. She'd never do that. "Your sister would never leave the family. Never."

"You didn't hear how she was talking. She's discovered a whole new side to her. She's had her nails done, her hair cut, she's glowing."

He'd noticed. A tiny fissure formed in his heart, and little pricks of jealousy dropped like pins all over his skin.

He and Ashleigh were together again, but she had discovered a new lease of life, and she was enjoying freedom she hadn't had before. Meeting gorgeous Italian men, or charming French men, or any manner of European men who would be blown away by her, no doubt.

It would break his heart to walk in and see Ashleigh with someone. Not that she was that type of woman. She wasn't. She was loyal and lovely and beautiful and she had the biggest heart, but they had only rekindled their romance recently. Was it strong enough to withstand the attention of other men?

"You can go whenever you have a week or so free. She's still out there for another two months. You could even go for the last part of her trip and come home together," Eloise continued, talking with enthusiasm now that she had the idea in her head. "You could explain to her in person. That might be a better way to do it, Ford. Don't you see? With you there for support, it would be so much better."

He didn't want to sneak up on Ashleigh. He wasn't that kind of guy, but it would be a way to soften the blow about her family. So, for that reason, he started to consider it.

"You should go," Eloise urged. "Think about it."

And he did. His mind started conjuring up images of Ashleigh's smiling face when he turned up at her hotel and surprised her.

CHAPTER 22

"See?" Ginny said, as she stepped back into the kitchen having seen Ben out.

"See what?" Eloise continued wiping down the countertops and her mind was still on Ashleigh and how much she didn't know about the changes at home. She hoped Ford would consider her suggestion to spring a surprise visit on Ashleigh because that would prepare her better than to turn up and see for herself.

"See how much Ben has changed." Ginny looked hopeful, waiting with bated breath it seemed for Eloise's answer.

She smiled at Ginny, as if agreeing, but she was thinking about other things. "I hope Ashleigh won't extend her trip a third time." She'd told Ginny about Ashleigh wanting to visit Turkey.

"I hope not," said Ginny, lovingly cradling her bump. "I don't want her to come after the baby is born."

"No," Eloise agreed. "She'll never forgive us."

"How will we break the news to her?"

Eloise recounted the conversation she'd had with Ford, and her idea for Ford to surprise Ashleigh on vacation.

"He knows about me?" Ginny asked, her eyes like saucers.

"I'm sorry. It just … it just came out. He'd seen you and Ben together a couple of times and he asked me if you were back with him." Eloise's eyes fell to her sister's stomach. Ginny was wearing a loose shirt, but the gentle swell of her belly was apparent. Ginny was starting to balloon. Her face had turned a little puffy, and she'd started wearing elasticated pants. Ashleigh would know as soon as she saw her. She told Ginny her plan for Ford to break the news to Ashleigh in person.

"I'd rather tell her myself."

"She'll know the minute she sets eyes on you, Gin."

"It should come from me," Ginny insisted.

"But imagine what a big shock it will be for Ash to come back from a wonderful trip of a lifetime and then to see you."

Ginny looked downcast. "It's good news. She'll see that in time."

"Of course it's good news," said Eloise. "But it will still come as a shock to her, Gin." She walked over to her sister and placed her hand on her shoulder. "Think about it. This news has been surprising to me … even shocking, at times, and I'm living with you. Think about how Ash will feel when she returns and you tell her that you and Ben are back together, and that you're pregnant."

"It's not bad news."

Eloise had to be careful what she said and how she said it. "It will time take for her to absorb what you tell her, about Ben being a different man, and wanting to take on responsibility for you and the baby."

Ginny chewed her lip. "It doesn't feel right Ford telling her. Ash deserves to hear it from me."

Seemed like Ginny was going to dig her heels in. Maybe she ought to go ahead and break the news herself. "Well, then maybe you should tell her on our next video call."

Ginny was helping to put the dishes away and every so often she would stop and run her hand over her bump. "I'm not sure. Let me think about it." Eloise was happy to let Ginny take as long as she wanted. In the meantime, she hoped that her plan for Ford would go through. Ford missed Ashleigh, and her sister missed him. It would be a perfect surprise.

"You'll see, and Ash will see, that Ben is trying to make up for what happened. You both seemed to be getting on well."

Eloise was at a loss for what to say whenever Ginny championed Ben. He'd come over for dinner earlier and Eloise had braced herself for the evening.

A couple of glasses of wine had helped. "He was quieter than I remember," she remarked. The man didn't talk much, but often, in the past, when he'd opened his mouth it was to make a silly comment, or, much to her and Ashleigh's dismay, it had often been to put Ginny down.

"He has a lot to think about. He's different. He's kind and gentle," said Ginny. Eloise tried to ignore the unease that rumbled deep in her belly. He should *always* have been kind and gentle. "I hope so," was all she could manage.

"He is!" Ginny retorted. "I wish you'd give him a chance. I wish you'd try to see him the way I do instead of hating on him all the time."

Eloise counted to five silently. She didn't want to end up in another argument with her sister. "I don't hate Ben. I never liked the way he treated you and when I saw that photo of him ..."

"But it's never been proven that anything happened."

Eloise lifted her hand to her face. Dear God. Ginny still believed he was innocent, and perhaps there was a chance, slim as it might be, that the man was innocent, but even if he hadn't technically 'done' anything with the woman, it was still wrong.

It spoke volumes about his character, and even now Eloise could see that Ginny was blind to it.

"You don't give him a chance. Let it go. For my sake, for the baby's sake."

This was why she knew Ashleigh would have been better in handling this. Eloise had baggage the size of four suitcases. Emotional baggage that she couldn't shake. It gave her a black and white view of things, and in this case, it didn't help.

"Matt cheated on me, and yes, maybe that's why I have a black and white view of these things. Even now, I can't change the way I feel. I can't trust easily, and I'm sorry if that's what might be coloring my view of Ben."

Ginny rested the dishcloth on the side and folded her arms. "At least you acknowledge that."

"I didn't know that he was cheating on me, for the longest time, and when I look back now, I was living in a lie. I thought I was happy. I thought he loved me, I thought we had a wonderful marriage. I thought life was great, and then I found out and my world fell apart."

"How does that relate to me?" Ginny asked innocently. "You can't think that what happened to you will happen to me."

"I'm telling you my side of things, Gin. I didn't know what Matt was up to, but once I found out, I looked back on every day of our marriage with different eyes. I saw things differently. I was so happy with him, I didn't think he would ever do that to me, but he did, and after that I opened my eyes and saw him for the devious, sneaky, unfaithful man that he was."

"Ben's not like that."

Eloise sucked in a breath. "Yes," she said, because she had no words to counter Ginny's.

"How did you find out?" Ginny asked.

"I got suspicious at a party we went to, and then I acted on my suspicions. I checked his cell phone. It wasn't easy to do, at first. I don't sneak around spying on others, but so many people had looked at me strangely at the party, and I could sense that something was off. And then I saw how talkative he was with one of the guests. Turns out she was his friend's younger sister. It was a friend from work, so I have no idea how he met her or how long he knew her for or how things developed. It was probably better for my mental health to not know that. But I read the text messages. I saw the photos, and they were from her."

"Photos?"

Eloise's face heated as those images came to the forefront of her mind again. "Trust me. Words are one thing, but photos, they tell the truth. There was no doubt that they were having an affair. Something broke inside me that day."

She lowered her head, trying to let the bile in her throat go down. That time in her life had hurt her badly and even now she often had a physical reaction whenever she remembered it.

"Come here." This time it was Ginny who put her arms around Eloise and hugged her. "I'm sorry this has brought it all back for you. I'm sorry it's causing you pain, but Ben isn't that guy."

Eloise rested her head against Ginny's shoulder and allowed herself a moment of respite. "I hope he isn't. I'm sure he isn't."

But she didn't feel truthful saying it.

CHAPTER 23

$\mathcal{A}$shleigh paused and didn't immediately answer the phone when Ford's name flashed up on it.

When it continued to ring, and she could no longer ignore it, she took the video call.

"Hey." Ford sounded enthusiastic and looked way too happy for someone this early in the morning.

"Hi."

Every time she spoke to someone from home, her heart turned heavy. She wasn't sure what caused more pain; the idea of being back at home and assuming her responsibilities again, or no longer being free to travel wherever and do whatever she wanted with her time.

She was suspicious because Ford had been trying to sneakily find out where she was, right down to the hotel, and then wanted to know where she would go next.

She hadn't thought much of it at first, but then Eloise and Ginny had asked the same on their last video call. Later, Eloise texted and asked her where she was staying, specifically asking for the hotel name and address because she 'wanted to send her a surprise'.

Nothing had arrived, and it further heightened her suspicion. Anxiety swirled inside her when she hadn't heard from Ford. She hoped he wasn't attempting to surprise her; that he wouldn't show up unexpectedly.

If he did, it would throw her for a loop.

When she'd first mentioned her travels to him, around the time when they were starting to get back together, she'd sensed that he didn't want her to go, and when he'd found out about how long she was going for, she knew he wasn't too happy about it.

That had irked her about him, and about being in a relationship after having been single for so long. She'd never had to answer to anyone, apart from her sisters, and even then, answering to a partner felt different.

More restrictive.

She didn't like that. She hadn't liked it much before, and now, traveling by herself for months, fending off curious and interested men, she certainly didn't like the idea of having to explain her every move.

Ford turning up to surprise her would be the worst thing that could happen.

"How are you?" he asked.

"Great. You?"

The conversation was stilted, even for small talk.

"What's the weather like?" His question made her suspicious again.

"Hot, and sunny. Not much different from Whisper Falls, I imagine."

"And are you still at the Santa Caterina Hotel in Portofino."

"Wow. You remembered that well. Why so many questions?"

"I want to know, no reason." He gave her a smile that didn't reach his eyes and she could tell that she'd upset him.

"Let me show you the view from my window." Not wanting to have a disagreement with him, she turned her cell phone towards the window and showed him the view. The layer-cake houses and hotels, and in the distance, the sea filled with yachts.

"That looks inviting."

"Isn't it wonderful? I feel so free out here!"

"Free?"

Dare she say it? "Freedom," she chose her words carefully. "Being free to do what I want, when I want, without anyone questioning me."

"Are you referring to me?"

Maybe she'd sounded harsher than she'd intended. "No I'm saying that... that I like being free."

He bowed his head, and she knew at once that he was unhappy.

"I'm not talking about you, Ford!" She laughed, trying to walk back her words.

"No?" He didn't sound convinced. "Is there something you want to say but you're not saying it?"

She laughed, but there was a tenseness between them that was new. She didn't want to be nasty, but she also wasn't one for going along with other people's agendas out of a sense of politeness. Goodness knows she'd done enough of that for most of her life.

"I'd better get on with my day," he said, abruptly. "You probably have lots planned?"

"I do." She was about to tell him all about it when he told her he had to go and that he'd call her later.

And then he hung up

Ford drove over to Eloise's summer house, where Liam was working, wanting to have conversation without drama, for a change.

The conversation with Ashleigh had jarred him; he hadn't expected her reaction to be so tepid.

The smell of fresh paint filled his nostrils as he walked towards the sound of Liam's voice. It sounded like he was on the phone. Liam popped his head around the door, then gave him a thumbs up. "Yeah, don't worry. I'll see what I can do. Gotta go." Liam hung up and the men shook hands. "Hey, what brings you here?"

"You didn't have to finish your call on my behalf," Ford answered. "I was in the area, so I thought I'd come by and see how this place was getting along." He walked around, admiring the new lick of color, and the way the place now looked. This house, albeit small, had the most wonderful views overlooking the sea. Surrounded by acres of land, it had the best of everything. He hadn't paid much attention to it, but seeing it now, he was getting ideas. "I don't even recognize this place anymore."

"This one has been a real transformation. It's been a joy to work on. Looks like a different house altogether, doesn't it?"

"Sure does. You've done a great job."

"Thanks. It was easy to do. Nothing major. It only needed some cosmetic touches. "

"I can't believe Eloise left this place untended for so long."

Liam nodded. "She'll sell this place in no time."

"I'm not so sure she wants to sell it anymore. She's thinking about renting it." Eloise didn't seem so eager to run away from Whisper Falls. He wanted to think that the hunky construction guy he'd sent her way might have had something to do with it, but he had a feeling it was more to do with Ginny's baby.

"Renting it out?" Liam seemed pensive.

"Eloise was always in Hyannis Port, visiting her best friend. Any time she could get off, she'd be there, but she hasn't talked about that for a while."

"Maybe she had other things on her mind?"

She did. And Liam knew of those things, still, it would be gossiping to talk about that now, and wrong to be discussing it with Liam when Ashleigh didn't even know.

"Who's Alex?"

"Pardon me?" He peered at Liam, and shook his head. "Alex? No idea, why?"

Liam shrugged. "No reason. It's not important. Come and see upstairs. I've started the painting there. The views from the top are even more spectacular than down here."

Ford followed upstairs and looked around. Half of the upstairs was painted. He stared out of the windows, saw the flowers and shrubs painted along the canvas of green.

Stunning.

To wake up in the morning to this view, well, that would be magical.

He could rent this, or buy it, if Eloise changed her mind about that.

He'd moved into the family home where his mother lived, but she was so poorly now and doctors weren't hopeful. She was ninety-four years old. He was going to take care of his mother for as long as possible, but he had to think about later, and the family home was too big for him to live in alone.

Maddie only came home during vacation time and she had another few years left in college.

He needed a smaller place.

Eloise's summer house would be closer to Ashleigh but far enough. She seemed to have a thing about needing her space, and he wasn't sure that he could easily fit into her life. He also didn't want to rush into anything, but rekindling their romance after being recently divorced, maybe he was moving too fast?

Ashleigh didn't seem as committed as he was. He wasn't sure if it was the newness of their relationship, or the rekindling of an old love, or whether things felt stale, to her. Or different.

He was trying to not get reeled in so fast, and Ashleigh going away hadn't been a bad thing, but he missed her. He had only considered surprising her because Eloise had asked for his help.

That could work. "Hmmm. I might consider renting it from her."

"You?"

"I need to think about getting a place while I set up the new accountancy practice. No rush, but … this is pretty. I don't know if Eloise is in a rush. She doesn't seem to be anymore." He waited for Liam's response but Liam's face was impassive. "How about a beer?" he suggested because, goodness knows, he needed one.

"Sounds like a good idea."

CHAPTER 24

*B*en was over again, and Eloise couldn't face another evening with him.

He was over most evenings now and Eloise didn't like being in the house when he was around.

They rarely went to his parents' house. Ginny had gone over only once; Ben still lived with his parents, because he'd probably been too lazy to move into the house he'd bought with Ginny. She and Ashleigh had wanted Ginny to decide what to do with the place. Putting it up for sale being the most sensible option, but Ginny hadn't wanted to think about it.

And now that they were together, chances were they would move back into it. Ginny had mentioned that Ben's mother was keen to meet Eloise and put the past behind them, but Eloise pushed back on that. She didn't want to meet Ben's parents, or talk about the upcoming birth, and possible marriage, as if nothing had happened. She needed Ashleigh by her side for that.

If Ginny was trying to make Ben feel more at home, this was one evening when Eloise felt restless and uneasy. With the couple all cozied up on the sofa watching a romcom, it was the final straw. She couldn't even be at peace in her own home.

She stared out of the kitchen window and saw the summer house in the distance.

Liam was probably there now, working away. He hadn't texted her after that night when they'd last spoken, when she'd found Ginny and Ben in the kitchen, when Liam had discovered Ginny's secret and he'd waited outside for her to make sure that she was okay.

She was sure he'd heard Ginny being rude and referring to him as the handyman. But that was no excuse for going silent.

For her part, she'd been avoiding him, but only because she didn't trust herself to get close to anyone, and she was most definitely attracted to him. She'd deliberately stayed later than usual at work, then came home and had dinner with Ginny, and now Ben, too. Being around the newly reconciled couple who were now ensconced in one another's arms, she felt like a fifth wheel on a car. She didn't want to be cooped up in her bedroom like a miserable teenager, or watch TV with them.

There was only one place to escape to.

It was time to face her fears, instead of choosing avoidance. Just because she'd been hurt once didn't mean she had to run scared for the rest of her life.

There was something about Liam Reynolds that pulled her towards him.

She made her way over there, walking across the field which separated them, her heart beating like a steel drum.

As she reached to pull the door open, Liam pushed it from inside.

It seemed that he had finished for the day. She stepped back in surprise, their gazes holding. Something pitter pattered in her chest. "You're leaving?" she asked, even though it was plainly obvious.

"I didn't know you were coming over."

That voice. Those eyes. That beard. A shiver rolled over her. "I haven't heard from you in a while."

"I haven't heard from you." The hard edge in his voice threw her off kilter and she wondered if he was leaving to go somewhere? With someone?

"I finished painting another room upstairs and it seemed like a good place to stop."

"Oh." The weight of disappointment echoed in her voice.

"What are you doing here?" He kept his hand on the door, keeping it slightly ajar, making her think that maybe he wasn't so eager to leave. A girl could hope. "I came to talk and see how it was going."

He swiped a hand through his hair, and she sneaked a quick glance at him, trying to tamp down her admiration.

"I'll have the painting finished soon, maybe need a week or two then I'll need maybe a week to finish the rest of it. And then it will be done. Completed to time and budget." He looked proud of himself, as if he was pleased with his effort and even more pleased to be finished and leaving. That's not what she wanted, and she hated that he looked as if he did.

And he hadn't answered her question. He'd taken her literally, thinking she was asking about the house. She wanted to know how things were with him. "I… I wanted to get back to you about the other night."

"The other night?" He frowned, and was acting strange and closed off, as if he hadn't thought about that other night like she had. Her heart sank, like a stone thrown into a river. Maybe he didn't have feelings for her; nothing like the ones she was starting to have for him. "You're annoyed," she stated.

"I'm not."

"About the other night," she said again, her mind racing to figure out what might have irked him. "I'm sorry I didn't get in touch sooner." She was afraid of being vulnerable, afraid of stepping out of her comfort zone, but that wasn't something she could tell him, not yet, while things were so fragile and the special chemistry she'd once felt between them was now tenuous.

"Don't apologize. You don't owe me anything." He nodded towards the door. "You can look around upstairs if you like."

"You're not going to give me a special tour?"

"I'm not."

She wrung her hands, her insides a mix of fear and anger. He would walk away soon enough and she had to make her stand. "You *are* annoyed. I'm sorry if you felt I was ignoring you."

He looked away, the muscles flexing along his jawline. Making her heart dance. She hadn't admired a man's face like that ever. But these days, she was mostly dreaming about Liam's biceps, or his broad back, or the way he filled out his T-shirt, or the way his eyes bore into hers occasionally.

"I like coming here." She didn't care to hold back.

"Why's that?" he asked, his voice sharp like a knife.

She opened her mouth. This was the part where she normally held back and kept careful watch over her words, did what it took to hide her feelings. Opening up to and trusting someone meant getting hurt and she didn't want to get hurt again, but there was something different about this man, something that made her think about him more than was good for her.

She was going to say it and speak the truth because secrets, as she knew only too well, made things worse. "Because... it's... it's a good distraction, coming here and seeing how the place is transforming."

"You like coming here to see how the place is transforming?"

"I like the company, too." She scratched her neck, because she never played this part. She was the wise-cracking, smart-ass, cold and detached girl who could have fun but only on her own terms. "You're a good distraction."

"A good distraction? Hmmm." Curious green eyes stared at her. He almost had a smile. *Almost.*

"From all the drama," she whispered, her voice breaking slightly. She was so not used to opening up. Cocktails, flirting and having fun were her thing, but life hadn't given her much of that lately. She sometimes felt adrift in a bottomless ocean and Liam was the lifebuoy that held her up. Liam who knew nothing about her but had only shown her kindness.

"The drama. Right."

Until now.

Clearly he was mad about something. Was it possible he was sulking because she'd stayed away from him? "I like you, but I'm scared of trusting people and—" But her cell phone rang, interrupting and stalling her. She ignored it and tried to continue, an untimely intrusion. "And ... letting them in." It was her boldest statement yet, and her heart clattered inside her, making her jumpy. "I don't know why I told you that—" she mumbled because the phone stopped ringing. Worse, Liam hadn't said a word and this wasn't the reaction she'd hoped for. She'd gone and exposed herself. A little voice in her head telling her that maybe he was already taken and she was assuming too much.

"Who's Alex?" he asked, and with the way her nervous heart was beating, the palpitations she was experiencing, she peered at him in confusion. "Alex?"

Her cell phone started ringing again.

"Maybe you should get that?" Liam suggested, his voice as cool as ice. His expression was cold and impassive and she felt like a fool for opening up to him when he hadn't even been affected by her words.

"Do you even care about what I'm saying?" She fished her phone out of her bag, saw Ginny's name, and answered. "Hey, Gin."

"Come quickly!" Ben's voice pierced her heart. The urgency, the fear immediately telling her that something was wrong. "It's Ginny. She's bleeding. I don't know what to do."

"Bleeding?"

Ginny? She froze.

Ginny was bleeding. Everything turned into slow-motion and in a daze she stared at her house in the distance, about to sprint across the field when Liam placed two strong hands on her shoulders. He gently turned her around. "What's wrong?" His eyes were filled with concern.

"It's Ginny. She's bleeding."

He grabbed her hand. "Come. I'll drive you there."

He drove like a fiend, fast and furious, like the chaotic thoughts shooting into her mind.

They were at the house in seconds, and she jumped out, keys in her hand, quickly letting herself in.

She raced to Ginny's side; her sister was curled up in a ball. Eloise dropped to the floor, taking in the blood on Ginny's dress, and the stains on the floor. Eloise dropped her head close to her sister's face. "Gin, what happened?"

Her sister whimpered, tears streaking her eyes. "I don't want to lose it. I can't lose it."

"You won't." She soothed back Ginny's hair and wiped her tears. Behind her she could hear the men talking. Liam asked Ben if he'd called 911.

"I was waiting for you. I didn't know what else to do," she heard Ben say. Eloise glanced over her shoulder and gave him her most hateful stare. "You haven't called 911?" she snarled, all her opinions about this man confirmed yet again.

Liam was already on his cell phone, talking to someone. He seemed shaken but in total control, and she was thankful that he was by her side.

"It's going to be okay, Gin. Do you want to sit up?" she asked tenderly, feeling scared and helpless and useless.

"It feels better lying down." Ginny's legs were tightly shut. Eloise had no idea what to do in such an emergency. Ashleigh would know, but she had no clue. She reached over and grabbed a cushion from the sofa before slipping it under her sister's head.

Liam placed a hand on her shoulder, then crouched down beside her. In a low voice he said, "The paramedics might take some time. Might be better if we take her. I can drive."

"Drive?" she asked, alarmed.

His eyes scanned her face. He nodded. "She's going to be okay. We can do it. We'll get there much faster if we take her."

"Let's do it. Grab some towels from the bathroom," she ordered Ben, who stood around looking like a confused tourist. It occurred to her then that he wasn't even comforting Ginny. Between her and Liam they slowly helped Ginny to a sitting position.

"I can carry her," offered Liam.

"Can you walk?" Eloise asked Ginny.

"I don't want to try."

"I'll carry her." Liam sounded insistent and he gently scooped Ginny into his arms.

They walked slowly to the truck where Ben was holding the door open. Eloise was furious, but waited until Ginny was inside. "*You* couldn't carry her?" she hissed at Ben.

"He offered first."

"She's your girlfriend, the mother of your child."

You useless, hopeless no-good waste of space.

"You take your car. I don't want Ginny to be squeezed in the truck." She didn't even wait for him to reply.

Ginny was checked over by the medical professionals while Eloise waited with Liam and Ben in the waiting room.

Liam would smile at her encouragingly each time she glanced his way, and she felt a little better every time he did that.

She hadn't forgotten the question he'd asked her, and it explained why he'd been so cold, but nothing mattered now.

Ben paced around the room feverishly, annoying her even more. She couldn't come to terms with the way he'd treated Ginny. Even when she lay on the floor bleeding, he hadn't called 911 and had called Eloise instead, then waited for her. He'd done nothing. He hadn't even offered to carry her to the truck. He was such a waste of time and space and once again, for the thousandth time since she'd gotten to know this man, she wondered yet again why her sister was still in love with him.

The doctor asked to speak to them outside and told them that Ginny had suffered from a condition known as placenta previa, and that she would require close monitoring and would need to take it easy. There was a strong possibility that Ginny would have to give birth by C-section.

"Is it fatal?" Eloise asked, sick with worry.

"No. We'll monitor her carefully and you just need to make sure she doesn't exert herself." Then he told them that they were going to keep Ginny overnight for observation and would let her go early the next morning if everything was okay.

"It's good news." Liam took a hold of her hand and

squeezed it gently. "She's going to be okay." When he put his arm around her she felt a sense of relief that Ginny was in good hands and the situation wasn't as dire as it could have been.

They walked into the room where Ginny lay, her face so deathly white, Eloise was in shock. She rushed to her side. "You're going to be okay, and the baby's going to be okay."

"Thank God," Ginny whispered. Ben stood on the other side of Ginny and took her hand. "It's going to be okay, babe."

No thanks to you. Eloise couldn't bring herself to look at him. She smiled at Ginny. "They're going to keep you overnight, for observation and if everything's good, they'll let you go home in the morning." In the back of her mind she decided that if all was well tomorrow, she wouldn't mention any of this to Ashleigh.

"I have to stay here?" Ginny wailed.

Ben kissed her hand. "It's for your own good, babe." Eloise waited for him to say something. Something appropriate. Something that might help redeem him from the lengths he'd fallen in her eyes.

"I'll stay with her through the night," she said to him, when he hadn't offered.

"I'll stay with you, keep you company, if you like," Liam said. Eloise turned to him. "That's very kind of you, but I think Ben is going to stay as well."

"I can't stay," Ben countered quickly. He bent down, lowering his head so that he was mere inches from Ginny's face. "I can't stay, babe. I have an early 5am shift tomorrow."

"You can stay up and go from here," Eloise suggested.

He stood up and eyed her. "I need to get proper rest, in a proper bed."

She fought the urge to slap him.

"You do understand, don't you, babe?" he asked, placing a kiss on Ginny's cheek.

"Of course I do."

"I'll stay," Liam insisted. Eloise didn't turn to acknowledge him or thank him, because she was so focused on giving Ben a dirty look. The contempt she felt for him was off the charts. She waited for him to leave, then sat down, still holding Ginny's hand. "We're going to stay here with you, Gin, but you need to rest now, okay? You've had a scare but everything's going to be okay."

"Thanks." Ginny gave her hand a gentle squeeze.

"He's a selfish guy, but don't let him get to you." Liam whispered in her ear quietly, so that Ginny wouldn't hear him. She nodded.

"Thanks for staying, Liam." Ginny whispered weakly. Her eyelids were starting to flutter shut.

"Don't mention it." He pulled up a chair next to Eloise but a good few inches away, so that he wasn't too close. Her heart melted. He was so good. So good. He was a perfect gentleman. A good friend. He was always there when he didn't have to be, and he was so much the opposite of Ben.

She felt sorry for her sister, and fearful for the future with Ben, but she wasn't going to waste any time thinking about that man. She'd wait for Ashleigh to return and between the two of them, they'd figure something out. A future where Ginny and the baby were taken care of, given that Ben seemed to be lacking.

"I'm so tired," Ginny murmured.

Eloise let go of her sister's hand. "Then go to sleep."

It wasn't long before Ginny seemed to be in a deep sleep. Her breathing long and deep.

"Why don't you try to nap. I'll keep an eye on Ginny."

They'd been sitting in silence for so long, and yet it didn't feel odd or awkward. It felt nice and familiar, like an old dressing gown.

"Why would you do that?" she asked, wondering why he had offered to stay the night with her.

"Because she's your sister and you're obviously stressed out. It's emotionally draining and you need your rest."

"What about you? Don't you need your rest?

"I'm good. I'm working for a very kind and understanding client at the moment, and I don't have her worries. I'm trying to be supportive."

She nodded, letting the words sink in. "You asked me about Alex."

"That's not important right now."

"But I can explain." She glanced at Ginny who was still asleep.

"I don't need you to explain, not right now."

"But—"

"Want me to get you something to eat or drink?" he asked. He really didn't want to talk about Alex and she was desperate to tell him. He must have heard the name in a conversation or something.

She was thirsty. "Could you get me a bottle of water, please?"

CHAPTER 25

Ginny opened her eyes and gasped in shock as she looked around the unfamiliar room.

Then she remembered, and quickly put her hands under the thin blanket, then moved them lower down, between her legs.

It felt dry.

She pulled her hands out and examined them, and only then did she exhale.

There was no blood.

It was going to be okay.

Her baby would be fine.

In a flash it all came back. last night, how she and Ben had been watching TV, how she'd gone into the kitchen to get a glass of water and felt a warm trickle of liquid down her leg.

Another snore grabbed her attention and brought her back to the present. Eloise was sitting almost halfway down the chair, in what looked like a very uncomfortable position, with her head bowed to the side, and snoring.

Not too loud, but still loud enough.

"Hey. How are you feeling?"

Her gaze shifted to the other chair, a little distance away from Eloise. It was the handyman, Liam. He gave her a polite nod. Liam was the one who'd offered to stay the night with her and keep Eloise company. Liam, not Ben. But she understood. Ben had an early morning shift. He needed a good night's sleep.

She shifted herself upwards a little. "I'm feeling better, thanks. I feel rested."

"Good. You slept soundly."

Ginny stared at her sister. "Has Eloise slept through the night?"

Liam winced. "Don't tell her, but, yeah. She pretty much did. She was fighting it for the longest time, though."

"She's tired." Ginny felt sorry for Eloise and was glad that she was resting. She lowered her voice as Eloise continued to snore. "Don't wake her."

"Not planning to."

"I'm sorry for keeping you here all night." She was grateful that this man, a stranger almost, had chosen to stay at the hospital.

"You didn't keep me."

Ginny's gaze bounced between Liam and her sister. "I know why you did it, and I appreciate it all the same."

"I had a feeling this might happen." He waved a hand at Eloise. "I didn't want there to be no one awake in case you needed something."

She gave him a knowing smile. "I see the way you look at her. I see how she goes running over to the summer house to 'help you.'"

He sat upright, as if he was getting fidgety. "I'm not sure I understand what you're saying."

"I'm sure you do."

"You referred to me as the handyman once."

"I'm sorry about that. I've got a lot going on and I've not been kind to Eloise. This isn't easy for her either."

He swiped his hand across his cheek. "I'm not so sure your sister comes to help me, as much as she's looking for a distraction."

His words made Ginny chuckle. "You're most definitely a distraction."

"I'm sure I'm not the only one."

At first she wasn't sure what he meant, but then she remembered she'd made a deliberate comment once. "Whoever you think she might have been interested in, she's not. She didn't go to Miami. She hasn't talked about wanting to go away for a long time. I'm not even sure there was anything there to begin with."

He seemed to be considering what she said, and she was pleased with herself for letting him have that information. "I don't know what she's told you, but she doesn't open up to people easily. She was hurt once, and she's been closed off ever since. I don't exactly know why she was interested in going to Miami, but she's not interested anymore."

He coughed lightly, his hand gripping the armrests. "You sure about that?"

"You could ask her. It takes her forever to get to the point, so you might want to ask her directly."

At that very moment Eloise let out a long, loud snore. Ginny's heart sunk. As her sister's wingwoman, she couldn't let this embarrassing matter continue.

Heaven forbid if Eloise started drooling from one side of her mouth. She clapped her hands loudly, waking Eloise with a start.

"What..." An embarrassing grunt followed as Eloise shifted herself upright, then looked around groggily. "What did I miss?" Then it must have come to her all at once because she was up with a jump, and at Ginny's side. "How are you feeling? Any pain? Any blood?"

"I'm okay. I'm feeling much better."

"Are you sure?" Eloise persisted.

"I'm sure. Stop worrying so much. We were only talking."

"We?" Eloise asked, confused. She really had been in a deep sleep. With her back to Liam she had completely forgotten that he was there until he announced his presence.

"Good morning."

His voice was a long, slow drawl as he got up. Eloise turned around as he stood up.

Ginny wished she could see the expression on Eloise's face, instead of the back of her head.

"You?" Eloise gasped.

Liam lifted his hand, hooked a thumb in the direction of the door, not once taking his eyes off Eloise. "I'll be back. I need to …" He was gone like a flash without finishing his sentence.

Eloise snapped her head back. "Did I snore?"

Ginny made a face. "It wasn't only the once."

Eloise looked grief stricken. "How loudly? How long?"

Ginny neatly sidestepped the question. "But you didn't drool." Her sister slapped a hand to her forehead. "Why didn't you wake me sooner?" she wailed.

"I did."

"Did he hear?"

"Do you care?" Ginny examined Eloise's reaction. Her sister looked as if she wanted to disappear into the floor. So, it was true. As she'd guessed, Eloise had a thing for the handyman. "You care what he thinks!" she exclaimed.

"I do not," Eloise retorted haughtily.

"You were snoring like a boar, and the spittle that was here," she pointed at the righthand side of her lips, "it dried up."

"You're lying," Eloise cried, clearly distressed.

"You care. You care a lot, and he cares about you, too."

Liam walked back in then, halting the conversation. The silence grew more pronounced and it was so painfully obvious that they were talking about him. He hovered around the foot of the bed. "I'll … I need to get back and I don't know when they'll discharge you," he said, looking concerned, as if this was something he was responsible for.

"That's okay." Eloise wiped a hand over her face. "You've done more than you should have and we're very grateful. Aren't we grateful, Ginny?"

"I already thanked Liam."

"It's okay if you need to go," Eloise continued. "We can always get a taxi back, whenever they discharge Ginny. Whenever that might be, who knows?"

Liam's mouth curved into a smile. "But if you're stuck, you can call me and I can come by. It won't take me too long."

Eloise put up her hand. "That… that won't be necessary, but thank you … for … for your service."

Liam's eyes widened. "My service?"

"For… for being here, all night, listening to… the sound of the… hospital…"

Ginny needed no further proof that her sister was in love because she was rambling. "Eloise is extremely tired. It's possible that she needs more rest than I do," she said, stepping in to stop Eloise from rambling like a lunatic.

Liam grinned and looked at them both in turn, then nodded, and left, closing the door behind him. Eloise slid back into the chair. "He's seen me at my worst," she moaned.

"You weren't drooling," Ginny said, not wanting to cause Eloise more stress than was necessary.

"Thank God."

"But you were snoring so loudly I thought there was a tractor in the hospital grounds."

~

Ginny had been discharged.

They'd come home around noon and Eloise instructed Ginny to do nothing but rest. But secretly she was worried about Ben's behavior. Not only had he left her, but he hadn't even called her today to see how she was.

Ginny had been the one to text him, to let him know that everything was fine and that she was back at home. When Eloise complained about his behaviour to her, Ginny didn't like it.

"He's tired. He works long shifts at the factory, and he does a lot of overnight shifts because he gets paid a little more. We need the money for the baby."

"You make too many excuses for him." Eloise tried to bite her tongue but it was impossible. Ben hadn't changed, and Ginny didn't see his faults.

"You're being too hard on him, like always. I wish you would understand that he's working hard to provide a better future for us."

Rage inflamed Eloise. Her nostrils flared. "You were bleeding. You're pregnant, with his child!"

"Stop! Just stop." Ginny wailed. "I don't want to hear this. I'm supposed to be taking it easy."

"I'm sorry. You are meant to be relaxing but," she couldn't help herself, "Ashleigh would be as worried about you as I am."

"I wish she were here."

Eloise sucked in a long hard breath. She couldn't get Ginny more upset, not in her present condition. "I'm sorry." Her voice softened to a whisper. "Don't worry. Ashleigh might come back sooner."

"I don't want to ruin her trip."

"I understand, but you'll be seven months pregnant then.

We owe it to her to tell her. Ford's thinking of going over to surprise her."

"He is? To do what?" Then Ginny gasped and put her hand over her mouth. "He's not …. He's not going to propose, is he?"

"No!" Eloise gulped. Who knew. Maybe that was his motivation. "Maybe."

"Ashleigh getting married," said Ginny in a dreamy voice.

"I said 'Maybe', but I don't think so. He just misses her, and this can be his way of helping us."

"How?"

"By going over he can tell Ashleigh in person. She needs to know, Gin. We can't keep this news from her forever."

"But it's my news to tell."

"You tell her, then. You were supposed to weeks ago, you said you wanted to tell her and you'd think about it. This way, Ford can go over and be there when you pluck up the courage to tell Ashleigh on a video call."

Ford had told her that he'd booked his ticket and was planning on going in a few weeks' time.

Eloise hoped that it might be enough to convince her sister to come back earlier. With another two months to go before Ashleigh returned, and with the way things were going at home, she couldn't handle more drama.

CHAPTER 26

*E*loise gazed out of the kitchen window at the summer house in the distance, and wondered what Liam was up to.

He'd called soon after Ginny had arrived, but she'd been busy with the laundry and their conversation had been quick and factual.

"Hey!" She heard Ginny's voice.

"Look at you! How are you feeling?" Shivers scampered along her back at the sound of Liam's voice.

She rushed out of the kitchen to see Ginny and Liam with their backs to her, walking into the living room. She tried to calm herself down, trying to remind herself that he'd come to check in on Ginny.

"Hi," she said, a little too breathlessly.

"Oh, hey." He took off his ball cap and gave her a captivating smile which she would replay again in her head many times when alone in her bedroom.

Then he turned to Ginny again. Watching them talk, Liam telling her he was glad to hear she was okay, and Ginny giggling like a schoolgirl with a crush, Eloise wondered when they'd gotten so friendly. Then Ginny's phone rang and she fished it out of her pocket. "It's Ben!" she cried, before disappearing up the stairs.

"So," Liam stood up as if he was about to leave. "How are you doing?"

She tucked a stray hair behind her ear and prayed her face didn't look too greasy from the cooking she'd done earlier.

"She's good. She's resting."

"I meant you. How are you doing?"

"Oh, I... " She tucked the same piece of stray hair behind her ear again. "I'm doing okay."

"Just okay?"

She had no answer for him, especially given that he seemed to be talking to her with a little more familiarity than usual.

"Thanks for coming by to check in on Ginny, and thanks for taking her to the hospital yesterday, and for staying there all night."

"You don't have to thank me."

"I do. You went way above what was expected of you."

"You said you're scared of trusting people." His eyes were like heat rays, because she felt a laser beam of heat all over her skin.

"Oh, that..." That night she'd overstepped her mark and wandered away from her comfort zone.

"I feel like we were at the start of a great conversation and then we got side lined."

She rubbed her arms, even though it was more than warm inside. Goosebumps sprang up of their own accord. Him talking about 'we' made her feel anxious and ready to take that jump off a cliff with him. "You asked about Alex."

"I did."

"He was someone I met at my friend's wedding."

"Someone special?"

"No. It was nothing serious."

"Okay."

"Okay," she said, breathing a little easier.

"I'm sorry I was so cold before." He turned the ball cap around in his hands. "I didn't want to step on Alex's toes."

"You're not."

"Good to know."

She felt a heaviness lift from her chest.

"Your turn."

"My turn?" She was confused.

"You've been avoiding me."

"Yes," she confessed.

"You don't trust people," he said, staring at her earnestly. "I respect that. I understand that trust has to be earned."

She heaved out a sigh. "My ex-husband cheated on me, and I've never gotten over that feeling of betrayal. I can talk to people superficially, but opening myself up to someone, that's scary."

He rolled his lower lip with his teeth, staring at her lips, his eyes darting all over her face as if he was slowly taking in her features inch by inch.

"I don't want you to be scared, but I understand why you are. And, just to put it out there, I like you, too."

The space between them filled like a sea full of possibility.

Ginny's laughter floated down from her bedroom, and Eloise couldn't help but roll her eyes. "Ben," she whisper-hissed. "It worries me that she can't see how useless he is. Is it me? Or would you agree?"

"Oh, he's very much an asshole." A look of disgust flashed across his face. "What he's doing is completely out of order."

"I have to tread a fine line. I don't want to upset her, but she can't see that his behaviour is not that of a caring man. He's already hurt her once and I can't bear to sit and watch while he does it again. I keep telling myself that he'll change, but he does so many despicable things. If you hadn't been around when Ginny started to bleed, I don't know what we would have done because Ben was of no help. It's only because of you that we managed to get her into the truck and take her to the hospital. I can't thank you enough."

"You can help me to finish the painting."

A smile spread out across his lips, and she found herself wondering what it would be like to kiss them.

A shiver ran across her chest.

"I can do that. I'll come over tomorrow."

CHAPTER 27

The Bridal Shop was closed by the time Ford finished looking at his new premises.

He'd found a nice little office to buy along Main Street. The perfect location and at a great price. It was still refreshing to see how much more affordable real estate was here compared to Boston.

But now he had an uneasy feeling in his stomach. What if Ashleigh didn't like the idea of him laying down roots here?

She might feel he was encroaching on her life, that he had ulterior motives.

He heaved a sigh, knowing this was ridiculous, that he and Ashleigh were so close, so in love before she left.

It was only the time and space that separated them.

But also, she had changed. She was enjoying her new freedom, and that thought now gnawed away at him.

He had to let Eloise know. He'd meant to do it a few days ago but his mom had been feeling poorly. Still, the shop was on his way home, so he stopped by.

When he peered through the window he saw Eloise deep in thought.

He hadn't missed her.

He knocked on the door and she looked up distractedly. A faraway look on her face, as if she had the weight of the world on her shoulders.

At least he wasn't the only one.

"Hi." She faked a smile as she opened the door. "I was about to go home."

"Then I was lucky to catch you."

She closed the door and looked at him with expectation. "When are you going?"

He rubbed the back of his neck, feeling bad that he had let her down. "I'm not going. I don't think it's a good idea, and now I've lost money on my ticket. The airlines don't give refunds for changing your mind."

"You changed your mind?" Eloise let out a groan and walked over to the red velvet chaise lounges. She sat down and removed her heels.

He hadn't expected her to be so devastated.

"She doesn't want me to come. I wanted to go, but your sister doesn't want me there."

"What do you mean she doesn't want you there? You were going to surprise her."

"Ashleigh isn't stupid. With you and me both asking her questions, she soon figured it out."

"No." It was a low, guttural groan, and when she plopped her elbows on her knees and covered her face with her hands, he was worried.

"I tried to surprise her but she had an idea that something was going on and then she gave me a speech about—"

"A speech?" Eloise moved her hands away and gaped at him.

"Yes, a speech. She told me she wanted her freedom and she

wanted to be free to do as she pleased, when she pleased and that she didn't want to answer to anyone."

Eloise frowned. She also looked a little different. He couldn't decide what it was, but she looked as if she'd done something different with her hair. Maybe parted it different, and she was wearing earrings. "Are you going on a date?" he asked, his curiosity getting the better of him.

"No! Why would you think that?"

He shrugged. "Look, I came to tell you that I'm not going."

She pressed her fingers across her brow. "Ashleigh can be direct at times, not often, but you shouldn't have let that put you off."

He snorted. Eloise was obviously desperate for him to go and break Ginny's news gently to her sister, but he wasn't about to turn up where he wasn't wanted.

It wasn't only what Ashleigh had said. She'd been a little cold. Slightly aloof. He'd lain awake that night trying to figure it out, and he believed he finally had.

She'd met someone.

"She doesn't want me there."

"How do you know?"

"I know!" He'd heard her. It wasn't just the words she'd used but the tone she'd said them in.

"Ginny had some bleeding."

"What? Is she okay? Is the baby okay?"

Eloise told him how they'd rushed her to the hospital, and what had happened there. "She's going to be fine, with a lot of rest and monitoring, but it's something else to worry about." She looked at him and the fear was there in her eyes. At last he understood her reaction.

He placed his hands on her shoulders. "It's going to be okay. I can't go because Ashleigh doesn't want me there, but I can pick her up from the airport and tell her then."

"She's not coming back for another six weeks!"

"Then either we tell her over the phone or ask her to come back sooner."

"Ginny doesn't want that."

"Ginny had a bleed," he countered. "Any number of things could go wrong. Do you still think it's wise to keep this from Ashleigh?" Eloise let out a loud sigh and he felt sorry for her. She slumped back against the red velvet backrest, looking distressed. "I will do whatever I can to make things easier for you and I'm always here for Ginny. Anything you girls need, just let me know. I'm sorry I wasn't there when it happened."

"Why would you have been?" she asked wearily. "We don't need rescuing, Ford."

He closed his eyes for the briefest of seconds. What was it with these women. The slightest hint of help and they were affronted.

"I wasn't planning on rescuing anyone. Not even Ashleigh." She'd made it clear to him, only, she hadn't specifically said it in as many words.

It made such perfect sense now. The only reason Ashleigh didn't want him to turn up unexpectedly was because she'd met someone. No wonder she was sad about returning home.

He'd rushed into things with her too fast. Her long vacation probably wasn't a bad thing in retrospect, especially if it made her see what it was she wanted out of her life.

He wanted Ashleigh to do the right thing by her, not by him. She owed that to herself.

"I can see you're upset, and I imagine the situation with Ginny is upsetting you even more. I think you should tell Ashleigh now, but, it's up to you."

"Ginny doesn't want to tell Ashleigh yet. She doesn't want to ruin her vacation."

He ground down on his teeth. Ginny wasn't looking at

things subjectively. Ashleigh would be furious. "I hope Ginny keeps well. Let me know what Ashleigh's flight details are for her return."

"Surely you'll have them? Surely she'll tell you?"

He wasn't so sure. "Just let me know, and I'll bring her home from the airport," he said quietly.

"It's still weeks away," Eloise groaned.

ord had given in too easily, and Eloise wasn't too happy about it.

But she was also confused by Ashleigh's reaction and wondered if Ford had read the situation wrong. She felt sorry for him because she sensed that he'd been looking forward to seeing Ashleigh, and that the thrill of a short vacation in Europe was not his primary motivation. It also seemed that Ashleigh's traveling adventures had changed her.

Feeling trapped herself, Eloise understood how that could happen. The idea of returning to Whisper Falls probably paled compared to visiting magnificent places, meeting new people and experiencing new cultures.

But Europe didn't call her in the same way as it did Ashleigh. Eloise harbored no dreams about traveling far. Even Hyannis Port no longer held any interest for her, but that was because her object of interest was right here, working away on her summer house.

As she arrived home after work in the evening, the sight of Ben's car outside made her heart sink. She walked into the house but felt as if she didn't want to be there.

"Hey, Gin." She acknowledged her sister who looked better and had had no further bleeding. Eloise glanced at Ben. "Nice to see you, *at last*." He nodded, lifting a can of pop to his lips, taking a sip, before letting out a contented sigh. "I've been working a lot."

Eloise wasn't going to let him get away with this so easily. She was still fuming by his apparent lack of regard for her sister. "Ginny was bleeding."

"I know, I was there." His tone was harsh, a warning note in it telling her to shut the hell up.

"You weren't there for long," Eloise countered.

"Stop!" Ginny hissed.

Reaching for Ginny's hand, Ben looked Eloise in the eye, hard and defiant. "You still don't think I'm good enough for Ginny. I couldn't care less 'cos I ain't got to prove myself to you or anyone else. Ginny and the baby are all that matter to me."

Eloise was about to open her mouth and throw something sarcastic at him when the fight went out of her. "How are you feeling?" she asked, looking at her sister.

"I'm much better now. I should be able to come back to work in a couple of days."

"No, you're not." This was the last thing Eloise wanted. "You're going to take the whole week off and rest some more."

"That's a great idea. Thanks." Ben leaned over and kissed Ginny on the cheek as if she'd been awarded a prize. "C'mon. Let's go." He tugged her hand and she followed like a faithful little dog.

"Where are you going?" Eloise asked Ginny, but Ben replied instead.

"I'm gonna treat her to a nice dinner."

Ginny giggled.

They were going out; she would have the house to herself. It was something to be thankful for. "Have fun." Eloise walked into the kitchen and breathed out when the front door closed. Gazing out of the window, she saw the summer house and longed to be there.

Just because she had the house to herself, didn't mean she had to stay here. She rushed out and half ran, half walked, eager to see Liam. To talk to him, and laugh with him, and to bathe in the low thrum of electricity between them. To feel the spark she felt when she was around him.

As she walked around to the front, her breath hitched in her throat. Liam had tidied the grounds, and though it was fall, he'd put two seats and a table on the porch. He'd made it homey, and by painting the outside, had given the whole place a fresh and clean look. This would be such a lovely place to sit and relax, especially in the summer.

It no longer looked like a run down and neglected place.

It looked like a home.

Not just any home, but her *home*.

Happiness flooded her insides and she rushed to the door, but before she opened it, she looked around. She could see herself here, waking up in the morning and looking out at the ocean. She could imagine herself sitting on the porch at the end of a long day and watching the sun set.

It was perfect. The front of the summer house looked onto the ocean, and the back of it was all that Ashleigh and Ginny could see. She liked that; it gave her some sort of privacy, and she also liked the idea that she was close by, yet still far enough away.

Feeling uplifted, she pushed the door open only to hear voices inside. When she stepped further inside, she saw a young girl, maybe in her mid-twenties, with her back to Eloise, talking to Liam who had his back to her and was fixing something on the wall.

Mid-twenties meant the girl was more than a decade younger than Eloise.

She felt a pinch in her chest. One that continued to turn sharper, and bigger the longer she surveyed the scene in front of her.

The girl was sitting on a stool, one leg dangling, the other resting on the horizontal bar. Dressed in denim dungarees and a white tank top underneath.

She was laughing.

They were laughing.

They seemed familiar.

It was uncomfortable for her to see. Eloise wanted to turn around and run, but it was too late. As if he'd sensed she were here, he turned around and looked right at her. "Hey."

Eloise kept her eyes firmly on Liam, but the girl turned around to look and Eloise could feel the weight of her curious stare.

"Hi." Her voice was strained, almost robotic. A hint of betrayal twisting like barbed wire inside her gut. All the excitement that had been bottled up inside her leaked out like air from a balloon. She'd been ready to praise him for what he'd done to the exterior, and was going to tell him that she no longer wanted to rent or sell this place, but was thinking about living here herself, but she couldn't say any of that now.

"Don't just stand there. Come in." Liam walked towards her, and she could see the question in his eyes. His confusion at the way she was behaving. She kept the door ajar, her heart in her throat, urging her to flee.

"This is Summer." Liam nodded in the young girl's direction.

"Nice to meet you." The girl smiled at Eloise.

"Hi." Eloise forced another smile. Her life lately seemed to be full of forced and fake smiles.

"I was going to call you," Liam said, speaking to her as if she was the only one in the room, throwing her off balance with his tenderness.

"Why didn't you?" She kept her voice neutral, her face expressionless even as a fire raged inside her. Could men never be trusted? Their last conversation had been so deep and meaningful, and she'd started getting ideas. Feelings intensified. Her emotions a rollercoaster of not knowing.

And now this.

"I was waiting for you to get back from work. I know how busy you get over there."

"Well, I'm here now." But she wasn't sure she believed him. Suspicion and doubt seeded in her head. From, the corner of her eye, she saw the girl slip off the stool and disappear into another room.

"Is there a problem?" he asked, appraising her. But before she could think of what to answer, the girl came back with a bottle of water in her hand, and wearing a jacket. "I'll bring it back in an hour." She dangled the keys to the truck in front of Liam.

"Drive carefully."

"Nice meeting you." The girl tipped her head at Eloise and walked out of the door.

"I should go." Before she humiliated herself again, she walked towards the door and opened it, but Liam pressed his hand against it, preventing her. She looked up at him in silent rage, her chest heaving.

"You came to see me."

"Because Ben was over." It was a little white lie.

"Oh, right. And that's the only reason you're here?" Thin lines fanned out from the corners of his eyes.

Liam had been her comfort and the summer house her escape from her recent stresses. But this would soon end, and it was probably for the better. He had a girlfriend, someone younger, sexier, gorgeous. Someone who made her feel old, frumpy and wrinkled in comparison. It hurt, and she didn't want to feel hurt. She wanted to be happy, and that's what she'd started to feel with Liam, but he was like most other men.

He had options. Probably lots of them. If he'd shown her any attention it was because he was working for her, and wanted to keep her sweet so that she would recommend him to others in the future.

Meshed with all the other little problems in her life, it was one thing too many.

"Please move your hand." Her voice was wobbly, betraying her.

"You came for a reason."

"To see how you were getting on."

"And yet you've been in a bad mood and you haven't asked me how I was getting on."

She ground down on her teeth, wondering what it was about her that made her a magnet for cheating men. "I didn't know you had ... a friend with you."

She had always assumed it, but she'd never outright asked him if he was single.

"Are you jealous?" His voice was tinged with mocking and it irritated her.

"Let me go, Liam. Don't be so annoying."

"You look nice."

If any three words had the effect of making her stop and falter, it was these three.

"W-what are you t-talking about?"

"You." His eyes twinkled. "You look nice. That was my sister, by the way. In case you were wondering."

She scoffed. "I wasn't wondering."

"No?"

"N-no." She coughed, tried to swallow because her mouth had turned dry. Now she felt like a real loon. "Why did she take your truck?"

"To help her boyfriend move out of his current place."

Oh, thank goodness. He sounded as if he was telling the truth.

He took her hands and looked deep into her eyes. "I'm not a cheating type of guy. It's not in my DNA."

She held her breath, needing to hear his words. "Okay."

"You look nice." He ran a finger over the sleeve of her blouse, making her jolt. "Thank you."

"My work here is almost done," he said, his voice sounding gravelly.

She'd been thinking about that, and dreading it. "You'll be going soon." She had sensed a finality in the air. The house was almost finished, all that remained was to buy furniture for it, but that wasn't Liam's job. "I don't want you to go." She sounded weak and pathetic, and needy, too. But it was true. She didn't want him to go. He would be out of her life soon, and there would be no reason for them to meet. He had no idea how much she looked forward to seeing him, to getting away from her life and working on this new home.

He peered at her. "No?"

He'd been a splash of light and happiness during these shaky, uncertain months and it was in moments like this, when he was so close to her that she felt dizzy, that she didn't want to face the void he'd leave behind.

She inhaled the scent that was so him; something she'd slowly absorbed and ingested, a smell that would always remind her of him. Earthy, clean and strong. No hint of flowers or the zesty sharpness most men went for.

"Problem is ..." His voice turned hoarse and he moved another step closer until he was no more than a few inches from her. She could feel, or maybe she was imagining it, the heat from his body.

"There's nothing else to work on," she offered weakly, in a voice that sounded hollow.

"That's not the real problem."

She stared up at him. "Then what is?"

"That I don't want to walk away and never see you again."

The words had just about settled on her when he leaned forward and pressed his forehead against hers. A thousand butterflies fluttered inside her belly. He touched her face, tenderly, delicately, as if she might break if he applied force. "You're really quite cute—"

"Cute?"

"And sweet, underneath that stony armor." He smiled, and it made her smile. It happened slowly, the way he seemed to shift closer, and she, mirroring him, did the same, enjoying his soft caress as he thumbed her lower lip.

And then he kissed her.

It was warm like summer rain, soft like a baby's touch. Sweet and tender. She groaned softly, and then he pulled away, and she stared at him, in a daze, feeling relieved and relaxed, as if a knot had been untied inside her.

She'd been thinking of this for days.

Might even have been weeks.

That pent-up frustration, the piled-on ever growing want.

"Did I move too fast?" he asked, his gaze dropping to her lips again as if he were considering another kiss.

Feeling flirty and bold, and well out of her comfort zone, and hopelessly, ridiculously attracted to him, she acted on instinct. "I'm not sure." She tip-toed up again, so that this time he didn't have to crane his neck too much. "Try again?"

The corners of his lips quirked up slightly, and then her eyes slammed shut as his lips pressed against hers once more.

Swoon.

His smell, his touch, his lips made her feel giddy and lightheaded and ready to fly.

"So, are we good?" he asked, his hands around her waist. She chewed her lower lip. "We are." She'd never felt better.

CHAPTER 29

The days were better after that. Life was good.

Eloise had someone in her life again. Someone good and kind. Someone who cared about her. They went out, on dates, for dinner, or to the movies, or for walks along the seashore.

One evening he surprised her.

He drove her further into the countryside, into the middle of a field where there were no buildings for miles around.

He spread out a thick blanket, and they lay down, looking up at the stars, wearing thick jackets so as not to feel the cold. Cozied up with him beside her, they kissed and talked and held hands. She felt like a teenager falling in love for the first time.

It was strange how summer had slipped away, and how different her life was now compared to when Ashleigh had left back in June. Life had changed for all the sisters. Ashleigh was on a trip of a lifetime, and Ginny would soon be a mother. As for herself, Eloise was no longer single.

Beth had called and wondered why she was so out of touch, and blamed Ginny for making Eloise's life hell. Eloise told her that the shop was busy and there was much to do, and promised to visit her over Christmas. But Beth and the fun life she represented no longer appealed.

This was what she wanted. This was what satisfied her soul, made her feel wanted, and safe and happy. Something as simple as lying on her back and staring up at the stars with the man who had walked into her life and surprised her. "I'm going to live in the summer house," she announced.

"What?" Liam turned on his side and lifted on his elbow. "What happened to your plans to rent or sell?"

"My plans changed." Like everything else around her. Things had changed from when she'd hired him to fix the place up. Her whole life was changing and she was wading into uncharted territory.

"Anything in particular happen to change them?" He traced her lips gently with his thumb.

She grinned. "I'm not sure. A certain handyman might have had something to do with it."

He bent down and pressed his lips to hers in answer. After the kiss he laid down beside her again.

"It's so peaceful and so remote here. I feel like it's just you and me in the whole world," she murmured.

"I like that feeling."

"Can we come here again, tomorrow? I love it out here."

"Can we come here again?" he echoed with a grin. "You sound like a kid saying that. How old are you?"

She sobered up, guessing that she was a few years older than him. Age mattered, and this shiny and delicate new thing they had needed to be nurtured and protected. "You make me feel like a teenager." She felt like a teenager saying it, but Liam had a way of making her feel things that had been long buried.

"Is that a good thing?" he asked.

"To this old dinosaur it is."

"You're not a dinosaur, and you're certainly not old."

"Hmmm."

"You're not," he insisted. "Are you … are you the type of woman who lies about her age?"

"No!" She sat up, outraged by his remark. "I've never lied about my age."

"You're acting weird about it."

She pressed her lips together, wishing they'd never veered down this topic of conversation. "I'm thirty-six."

"I know." For a split second he looked as if he'd revealed something he shouldn't have. "I'm thirty-three."

"How do you know I'm thirty-six?" she demanded. "Did you ask Ford?"

He looked unsure, and the longer he was silent, the more worried she became. "Did you ask Ford?"

"No." He let out a sigh.

"Then?" An inner alarm bell went off in her head and she shifted away from him a little. "You're not telling me something." His reticence reminded her of the times she'd questioned her ex-husband after her suspicions had been aroused.

He sat up slowly, before locking his arms behind his neck and heaving out a long breath. "You were three years above me in high school."

She gasped. "We went to the same school?"

"You were a cheerleader."

Her mouth fell open.

"I noticed you from the moment I walked onto the field and saw you practicing?"

"You knew me?" she asked slowly, her mind going back to her high school years as she tried to remember.

"I knew of you."

"But I don't remember you," she cried.

"That sounds about right. You never looked my way."

"I'm sorry." She tapped her fingers on her head, desperately racking her brains, trying to recall something, anything, but she couldn't. "I'm sorry. I don't remember you at all."

"It's okay. I figured you wouldn't." He shrugged. "Don't worry. I haven't been pining for you for years, or ever," he said quickly. "Ford told me you needed some work done on your house and he mentioned it was one of the Rose sisters, the ones who run the bridal shop, but I already knew. He told me it was 'Eloise, the middle sister,' and I knew it was you."

"You took on this job because of me?

"I took on the job because I could do the work." He paused a moment. "I had a crush on you back in high school, and I had a chance to see you again so …"

Oh my God. Oh my God. Oh my God.

He moved away, as if he was afraid he'd said something out of place. "I realize how this might sound, now that I'm saying it out loud. I'm not stalking you, Eloise. I haven't been pining over you."

He looked sad, and that big, strong demeanor of his seemed to evaporate. He'd had a girlfriend who'd died, and he, too, had been hurting.

Poor man.

She moved towards him then sat on her heels, and gently stroked his face. "You had a crush on me all those years ago?"

"I did."

Her heart melted. "That's the nicest thing to happen to me in a long time."

"You think it's weird?"

"No." This was a love story, of sorts. She traced his lower lip with her finger, then kissed him.

"You don't think its creepy?"

"No!" She framed his face with her hands.

"Because you looked worried."

"No. I'm not worried. I'm touched that you … liked me back in high school. I still can't believe it."

He answered her with a kiss. "Believe it."

She laughed and threw her arms around him and they sat like that in the dark, quiet of the night.

"C'mon," he said, after a while. "We should go. It's getting late." He helped her down, and quick as a flash, his hands went to her waist and stayed there. "I like having you around. I like *this*."

He wasn't afraid to share his feelings, to say what he felt, and she liked that. And the cherry on top? This man had liked her since high school. That had to be the biggest boost to her confidence.

Liam Reynolds had taken this job knowing that he'd get to see her again. And she'd had no idea of who he was.

They kissed again, a ripple of desire rolling over her. She sat in the truck, grinning like a loon as he drove back to the house. And it was only when they pulled up, that she saw the open door, and saw Ford's truck pull up outside their house at the same time.

"What the..." She fished her phone out of her bag. She'd had it in the truck when they'd been lying outside, and she saw, to her dismay, that she'd had thirteen missed calls from Ford. She'd put her phone on silent mode.

"Damn it." Liam growled. "My phone died earlier. I didn't even realize until now."

As soon as Liam pulled up, she rushed out towards Ford, bracing for the bad news.

Something had happened to Ginny, or the baby.

"Been trying to get a hold of you both." Ford's worried gaze swept over her and Liam.

"What is it?" Eloise's heart plummeted. If something terrible had happened to Ginny, Eloise wouldn't forgive herself.

Liam wrapped his arm around her shoulders, pulling her into him.

Ford looked glum. "It's Ben. He's been in a car accident."

A car accident?

Alarm bells went off in her head. It meant only one thing.

Ginny.

She felt the contents of her stomach drop. Ginny would have been with Ben. "Noooooo!" she cried, stumbling back, as if she'd been punched. "Not my Ginny," she wailed, her frenzied cries piercing the silence of the night as her world shattered into tiny shards.

Ford grabbed her shoulders. "It's not Ginny."

"W-what?"

"It wasn't Ginny in the car."

It took a few moments for that to sink in. "She wasn't with him?" Her shoulders stooped as she crumbled forward with gratitude, and fell against his chest. "How's Ben?" she asked, when she had composed herself.

Ford's face turned ashen. "He's not good. He's not in a good way at all. There's something else …"

"What?"

Ford looked reluctant to tell them. "There was a female passenger with him."

"Who?" Eloise cried, not sure what to make of this news.

"Wait, what?" Liam echoed.

Eloise stared at Ford through tear-streaked eyes. "What do you mean it wasn't Ginny?"

Ford looked at the ground. "It wasn't Ginny in the car."

She opened the door to the house and rushed in. "Ginny!" She was about to run up the stairs when Ford grabbed her arm. "She's not here."

Ignoring him, she yanked her arm free and raced upstairs, her heart beating, relief and terror co-mingling inside her.

"Ginny!" She flung open the bedroom doors one by one, then the bathroom door, all the while yelling her sister's name, desperate to see her. She needed to make sure that Ford hadn't made a mistake and gotten his facts wrong.

As she flew down the stairs, she caught sight of Ford and Liam huddling together, talking.

"She's not here." Liam tried to reach for her hand but she flew past him and started searching around downstairs. "She's not here!" he shouted after her.

"She's with her friend, Talia," Ford said, as she stepped back into the hallway. "I called Ginny as soon as I heard about Ben. I was trying to get a hold of you first, then I tried Liam but I guess you guys must have been busy." He coughed lightly, not meeting their gazes.

"How do you know it was Ben?" None of this was making sense to Eloise. Hands on hips she glared at Ford, hating him for bringing the bad news.

"I saw the wreckage on the road and knew it was a bad accident. I called someone I know at the hospital and they told me. Rumors spread, even in a hospital."

Eloise frowned, knowing that in a place like Whisper Falls, news spread quickly. She couldn't think properly and her mind blanked. "Who was he with?" Disgust and loathing consumed her. She held her cell phone in her hand, not trusting herself to call Ginny because there was too much emotion in her voice.

There were too many questions in her head.

How was Ben?

And how was his passenger?

Who was his passenger?

Thank goodness Ginny hadn't been in the car.

Ginny, her little sister Ginny, who was with child. Liam took her by the elbow and got her to sit down. He managed to calm her and gave her a glass of water and brought over a box of tissues. Ford talked, and some of it went in. some of it made sense. A lot of it didn't.

Ginny was at her friend's place.

"I have to tell her. I have to..." A heavy feeling settled over her chest. She wasn't sure what would break Ginny's heart more, that Ben was in an accident, or that he was with another woman. She might have been a friend and nothing more. Eloise reminded herself of the mistake she'd made about Liam's sister. Maybe this female passenger was a friend, or a cousin, or some long distant relative of Ben's.

Maybe there was nothing to it.

Because right now her head was spinning with questions, and she didn't know what to tell her fragile sister.

"He's at the hospital. We should go there."

"But I need to tell Ginny."

"Then let's go to Ginny first." Liam crouched on the floor, earnestly staring back at her.

"Thank you," she whispered, feeling grateful that she had Liam to fall on because everything inside her felt lost and broken into pieces.

CHAPTER 30

"*E*loise?" Talia looked surprised.

Ford drove them both, which was just as well because she was a mess. She was vaguely aware of Liam's arm around her, and her face resting against his shoulder.

They reached Talia's house shortly, and Eloise braced herself.

"Eloise, hi!" Talia looked surprised to see her, but her face turned sombre.

"I need to speak to Ginny, please," Eloise said, trying to fortify herself. She couldn't fall apart now, but she felt hollow, and she was scared knowing that the news she had to impart would rip Ginny's heart to shreds.

"Are you okay? What's wrong?"

"I need to speak to Ginny. She's here, isn't she?"

"Sure, come in, I'll go get her."

But they remained where they were, on the doorstep, while Talia disappeared. It helped that Liam's hand was on the small of her back; a gesture of support, and a reminder that she wasn't alone.

It helped that Ford was next to her; his presence giving her much comfort. Ginny came to the door, her face creasing with worry when she saw all of them at the door.

"Something's happened," Eloise said, wondering if it might have been better to break this news while sitting down.

Ginny's hands went to her belly, as she leaned against the door, sheer terror in her eyes as if she was expecting the worst.

"What? What is it?"

"Let's go inside, shall we?" Ford's strong voice and sensible suggestion made sense and he ushered them into Talia's living room.

"Come and sit down, Gin." Eloise patted a space on the sofa.

"What?" Ginny whispered, her voice so quiet, Eloise knew she expected the worst.

"What's going on?" Talia asked.

Liam mumbled something but Eloise couldn't make out his words.

"It's Ashleigh, isn't it?" Ginny cried, covering her mouth with her hand.

"No! It's not. It's not Ashleigh, Gin." Eloise took a deep breath. It was better to say it out loud. Better to say it now. All in one go. "It's Ben. He's been involved in a car accident and he's been—"

"Ben?" Ginny rushed to stand, as she let out a wail.

"Sit down, Gin."

"I don't want to sit down!" Ginny screamed, her face turning white. "Where is he?" She cradled her baby bump.

"He's ... he's..."

"He's at the hospital, Ginny," said Ford.

Ginny collapsed onto the sofa. Fat tears rolled down her cheeks. "How is he?" She sat forward, looking so pale that Eloise was suddenly worried.

"He's at the hospital, Gin," she said quietly.

"But he's okay?" There was a pleading tone in Ginny's voice.

"I'm sure he's okay." Eloise stared down at her hands before taking in a big breath.

Ginny looked at her, then Ford, then Liam.

"What aren't you telling me?"

Eloise opened her mouth. She tried to speak but her mouth was bone dry.

"WHAT. IS. IT?" Ginny yelled, turning hysterical.

"He … he ... uh …" She couldn't form a sentence, for fear of breaking her sister's heart. Of ending the future Ginny had dreamed of.

"Is he alive?" Ginny cried, breaking out into sobs.

"Yes, he's alive … he's alive …" Eloise swallowed, then looked at Ford because he hadn't mentioned anything about the state of his injuries. "But … there was a passenger in the car."

"His mom or dad?" Ginny offered, her sobs subsiding.

Eloise's stomach turned to steel. "No. Not them ..." she managed to say.

"He had a passenger, a female passenger, and she's been injured as well." Ford stepped in, and Eloise was grateful.

"A female passenger?" Ginny looked at her baby bump and shook her head as if the news didn't make sense, or she was unwilling to believe it. "I told you," Talia said. "I told you and you wouldn't believe me—"

Ginny broke down into a fresh round of sobs, holding her head in her hands as she wailed. All Eloise could do was place her hand on her sister's back and be there for her. They let Ginny cry her heart out for a little longer. Eloise lost track of time. She had no idea how late in the evening it was. "Stop that now, Gin," she said after a while. "All that crying isn't good for your baby."

"Yeah, Ginny. Think of the baby," Talia cautioned.

"You warned me." Ginny sniffled, holding up a soggy tissue and attempting to wipe her nose with it. Eloise handed her a clean one, before mouthing, "You knew?" to Talia, who shrugged in turn.

Ford coughed. "I think we should head to the hospital, and check in on Ben. I'm not sure, Ginny, if you'd like to go?"

She looked up at him with bloodshot eyes. "I need to see him. He's the father of my child. We don't even know who he was with. He might have been giving someone a lift out of kindness." Her monotone reply seemed to suggest that she'd been piecing it together into an explanation that made sense to her. "I want to see Ben, now."

"Let's go," Ford said, and they all stood up to leave.

Ginny was in pieces, and trying to hold it together for the baby.

Their baby.

There had to be a mistake. Or some rational explanation.

But what if this was the truth?

Talia had tried to tell her, but Ginny hadn't wanted to listen to her. Hadn't wanted to believe her because she desperately needed everything to be fine. Eloise had warned her, and she'd treated her sister with contempt, because she didn't want to believe her, either.

She'd put all her faith in Ben, but the truth was out. He'd been with someone else. He'd had another woman in the car.

She wanted her happy ending even if others didn't see it that way. They didn't understand. She would soon have a baby, and she was scared about how she was going to raise that baby alone. It didn't matter what Eloise said, about her and Ashleigh supporting her. She didn't want to be a burden to her family.

She wanted her own family.

She wanted her happy ever after.

She hadn't gone to him. Ben had sought her out, and she'd been wary at first. Not trusting. Not wanting to have her heart ripped out and chewed to pieces like the last time.

But carrying a new life inside her had turned her soft and vulnerable. When she told him about the baby, he'd cried. He'd been so sweet.

She had truly believed that they could start again. That he would change. That Eloise was wrong, and bitter and twisted because of how her own life had worked out. Not all men were like Eloise's ex-husband.

But now this had happened. There might be a simple explanation for the woman in his car, and as long as Ben was going to be okay, as long as the other woman was going to be okay, then she would be fine.

But if there was another reason for him being with another woman, she'd never take him back. Never trust him again. She'd never trust anyone with her heart again. She understood, at last, why Eloise had been so hard with her.

Liam and Ford walked on ahead, and she was behind, with Eloise and Talia supporting her, their arms hooked in hers, as if they were afraid she would crash to the ground.

But as they walked from the hospital parking lot towards the building where Ben was, her heart was in her chest. Vicious thoughts circled her mind like screeching vultures.

It had been days since she'd met with Ben. She hadn't wanted to admit that Eloise was right, but after her bleeding, when Ben had stood by helplessly like a statue, she'd been hurt.

He'd worked the night shift that night, but he hadn't come to see her until late the next evening, and even though she pretended to Eloise that it was okay, it wasn't.

The doubts and suspicions had started once more.

He'd taken her out to dinner a couple of days later, but he'd been inattentive. Distracted. On his cell phone more than she'd liked. He hadn't shown her the type of concern she'd expected.

She avoided meeting him after that, choosing instead to go to Talia's house.

As they walked up to the reception desk at the hospital, where Ford and Liam were ahead of them, she was so caught up in her downward spiral of emotions, that the noise didn't at first register.

The screams and cries of a woman in anguish took a while to pierce her awareness.

Ford turned around and looked at her, then at Eloise. His face grave, and as he turned to the side, revealing the view he'd been blocking, she caught sight of Ben's mom in her husband's arms, holding onto him as if she had lost everything.

And that's when it hit her. That's when she recognized the wails of a broken woman.

And that's when she started to see dots in front of her eyes.

"Help!" Eloise cried as Ginny slumped and she and Talia had difficulty keeping her upright.

In a flash, Liam was there, scooping Ginny up in his arms.

There was a commotion at the front desk. Ford hollered that Ginny was pregnant, and nurses and doctors rushed to her.

They took her away, and that was when Eloise, knowing that Ginny was in good hands, walked over to Ben's parents, fearing the worst.

Ben's mother looked at her, her eyes red veined and her face bloated. "He's gone... " she wailed. She sucked in air, her shoulders shuddering, her body convulsing as she buried her face in her husband's chest and sobbed.

Eloise looked at Ben's dad as if not fully understanding, as if she needed more confirmation, but deep down she sensed the tragic news was real.

"Ben's... gone. They couldn't save him," his father said, before lowering his head and hugging his wife tightly.

Eloise felt her body go slack, and she stumbled backward, but something caught her, something strong and steady, cushioning her fall. It was Liam. His chest absorbed the weight of her body and his arms closed around her shoulders. "I've got you," he whispered, folding his arms around her.

"He's gone," she sniffled into his shirt. "Ben died."

She felt the press of Liam's lips against her head. "I heard. He passed a short time before we got here. We were too late."

She stayed like that, cocooned in the warm comfort of Liam's body for a long, sustaining moment, and then her thoughts went to Ginny. "Where's Ginny?"

"She's fine. She's being seen to." Liam took her hand in his and led her into the room where Ginny lay on a hospital bed. She looked broken, a former shadow of herself. A ghost.

Eloise reached for her hand and pressed it between both of hers. "I'm so sorry, Gin," she whispered, trying to hold back a sob. Trying to be strong for her sister who would surely fall apart.

Her poor little sister. Ginny had experienced so much heartache and tragedy in her young life. It was unfair. This girl had had heartache from when she'd been nothing but a toddler. First losing their parents, and now, the father of her child.

When was life going to give her a break?

"What am I going to do?" Ginny sobbed. "Ben's gone. I'm all alone." She broke into another round of sobs.

"You're not alone, Gin." Eloise kissed her sister's hand.

"My b-baby has n-no f-father," Ginny wailed, inhaling huge gulps of air as she tried to get her words out.

Eloise swallowed. There was nothing she could say to that. She squeezed Ginny's hand lightly, and watched her sister's fragile heart shatter.

CHAPTER 31

At some point in the night, Ginny stopped sobbing and fell asleep.

The doctors kept her in overnight for observation, especially because of her condition and they didn't want to take any chances. Eloise shifted in her hard plastic chair again. She hadn't slept at all, but now her body was bone tired and the hardness of the chair grew unbearable.

She'd told them all to go home—Ford, Liam and Talia. Liam had insisted on staying, but she told him he needed to get his rest because she would need to draw on his strength in the days to come.

She stayed by her sister's side all night. Ginny would fall asleep, then awaken, then cry, then fall asleep again in one vicious never-ending circle of exhaustion. Eloise barely slept.

The next morning, when Ginny had been given the go ahead to go home, Liam picked them up.

Later that afternoon, Darcie turned up, having heard about the accident, no doubt from Ford. "I can't believe what happened?" she cried. "Does Ginny know?" Eloise rushed her into the kitchen, since Ginny was in the living room, sitting on the sofa and staring listlessly out of the window.

Eloise updated her on the now old news that Ben and Ginny had gotten back together and that Ginny was heartbroken. Darcie was shocked. "They got back together? When?" then, "Why am I always the last to know about anything?"

Eloise told her and explained why they'd had to keep things under wraps, why they couldn't risk Ashleigh finding out. Darcie remained silent at first, her brow creasing as she tried to make sense of it. Hesitation danced in her eyes. "Ginny looks … a little more … *filled out* than usual."

"You think?" Eloise twirled a lock of her hair around her fingers. Ginny was now six months pregnant, and her height and voluptuousness could only cover so much. Darcie had sharp eyes, and there was a good chance most people knew. It was only Eloise's deluded thinking that made her believe no one would notice. Of course they would. Of course they had.

"You don't think?" Darcie asked haughtily. She walked out and then reappeared. "I snuck a peep at her. She's all covered up with a blanket, but she looks … not like her usual self. Is there something else you want to tell me?"

It was on the tip of Eloise's tongue. But she couldn't tell Ashleigh's friend before she told her sister. So, she changed the subject. "It's such tragic news about poor Ben. I don't know how to tell Ashleigh."

Darcie pressed her fingers into her forehead. "You haven't told her?"

"She doesn't know…"

Darcie looked confused. "That they're together? Or about Ben?"

"She doesn't know any of it."

"I'll ask you one more time." Darcie placed her hands on her hips like a mildly annoyed school principal who was giving her one last chance to come clean. "Is there anything else you want to tell me?"

Eloise could hear the blood pounding in her ears. She could feel the overbeating of her heart. She traced a finger on the countertop, avoiding, ignoring, burying her head and not wanting to answer another question. She was bone tired; she hadn't slept and she was starting to realize what a huge mess this was. And it had happened on her watch. She'd been in charge, and she was to blame.

"Ginny's pregnant, isn't she?" asked Darcie, when Eloise refused to say a word. "Isn't she?"

Letting out a sigh, as if she were releasing secrets, Eloise looked Darcie straight in the eye. "You didn't hear it from me." At least she could tell Ashleigh that she hadn't told Darcie. That Darcie had guessed, as had most of the townspeople, probably. Rachel and May likely had their suspicions, though they hadn't said a word.

Darcie let out a guttural gasp, before clasping her hand to her forehead in dramatic diva fashion. "All of this is going on …" She gestured with her hand towards the door, indicating Ginny. "She's pregnant, and back with Ben, and now Ben is … no more …" she hissed. "And Ashleigh. Does. Not. Know. *ANY*. Of. This?" Eloise shrank back from the matronly stare Darcie gave her. "It looks bad. I know. I *know.*"

"You can't know. What were you thinking? You weren't thinking. Ashleigh is going to explode when she comes back to this. *Why* didn't you tell her?"

Darcie's accusatory tone made Eloise feel awful. "It's not like…" She fidgeted, shifting from foot to foot, folding her arms, then placing them on her hips, then holding onto the back of a chair. "I wanted to tell her, but Ginny was adamant I didn't. She didn't want Ashleigh to come back. She didn't want to ruin her trip. We've had so many arguments. You know what Ginny can be like, and she and I don't have the best relationship. It's been so hard." She pulled the chair out and sank into it, putting her elbows on the table and burying her head in her hands. "I didn't not want to tell her, but it was such a battle to get Ginny to agree."

She felt the gentle squeeze of Darcie's hand on her shoulder. "I can see why you didn't want anyone to know, but it's not hard to figure it out now. How far along is she?"

"Six months."

"Six months and Ashleigh has no idea … about any of this?" Darcie's eyes grew large like golf balls.

"Sshhhhhh." Eloise put a finger to her lips.

Darcie groaned. "Ashleigh asked me to keep an eye on you girls, but I've failed."

"You haven't failed," Eloise told her, not wanting her to take any of this blame.

"I get it. I understand. I know the dynamics in this family, and I get how hard it must have been for you. I wish you'd told me. I wish I'd noticed. I've seen Ginny and I thought she was comfort eating because of the breakup. I had no idea of what was going on."

"It's bad, I know. I don't want to think about Ashleigh's reaction when she finds out," Eloise whispered. "I was hoping Ford would go over and tell her, but that plan didn't work out."

"He's not going?" Darcie eased into the chair next to her.

"He says Ashleigh doesn't want him there."

"What?"

Eloise was as surprised about it all as Darcie seemed to be. "Has Ashleigh said anything to you?"

"Not a thing."

"Eloise!" Ginny's weak voice carried into the kitchen.

"I should go." Darcie tapped her on the elbow. "Let me know if you need anything. I'm sorry about Ben. I'll pay my respects to his parents. I'm sorry for what happened, to Ginny and—"

"Eloise!" Ginny yelled.

Eloise huffed out a sigh. "See what I mean? I'd better go. She's so volatile at the moment."

"Understandably so." Darcie gave Eloise a comforting hug, then went to see Ginny and gave her a hug. "I'm sorry for your loss."

Eloise waited in the hallway, then saw Darcie out. "Call me if you need anything," Darcie told her.

"I'll need your support when we tell Ashleigh."

"When will that be?"

Eloise shrugged. "She's not due back for another six or seven weeks."

"That late?"

"She kept extending her trip."

"You're going to leave it that late? I don't think you should, if you want my opinion. You don't want Ashleigh coming back to a crawling baby."

"The baby's not due until January."

"You know what I mean." Darcie looked bewildered. "I did not expect this when I walked into this house."

"I'm sure you didn't."

"Eloise!" Ginny cried.

Eloise rushed into the living room, to her sisters' side. "What is it? Are you in pain?" Ginny was kicking up such a commotion that Eloise feared it might be something to do with the baby. Instead her sister handed her cell phone to her. "It's Ben's parents. They keep calling me."

"Are they on the phone now?" Eloise whispered, her heart sinking.

"No. I didn't take the call. They keep calling but I don't

want to talk to them. I don't know what to say to them. I don't know what they want to say to me."

Eloise felt the same, but she took the cell phone away. Ginny didn't need the extra stress of people calling. "Don't worry about this."

Poor Ben.

He would never see his child. Her heart broke for his parents. Ben was their only child and she couldn't begin to imagine the devastation they felt. No parent should ever have to bury their child. It wasn't the natural order of things. No matter what she thought of Ben, and the way he'd behaved, he didn't deserve this. Eloise's heart broke for him and for Ginny.

"Can you take the call next time? I can't deal with them yet."

"I'll talk to them," Eloise reassured her sister. But not yet. Even she couldn't deal with them.

"What?" Ginny asked, when Eloise hadn't moved away. There was something she wanted to tell Ginny, news about the other passenger, the female in the car with Ben. She'd only broken a leg. Whereas Ben had lost his life. She wasn't sure whether it would be a good thing to tell her sister yet.

"What?" Ginny insisted.

Maybe the news might help Ginny to cope. To know that the other passenger didn't have fatal injuries. "It's about the… the… passenger, the one who was in the car with Ben. It looks like she's going to be okay."

Ginny turned her face away. "I'm glad she didn't die, but I don't want to know anything about her."

"At least you weren't in the car, Gin. Imagine if you had been, and the baby …"

"Is that meant to make me feel better?" Ginny snapped. "That I wasn't in the car but another woman was?"

Eloise had hoped it might help. It was another way of looking at the situation, but Ginny was too angry, and too upset. "Get some rest. I'm going to stay at home with you for the next few days."

"Who's going to run the shop?"

"We have Rachel and May. They'll manage."

CHAPTER 32

$\mathcal{L}$iam came by the house every morning to check in on Ginny, and then he would take Eloise into another room and hold her hands, and ask her how she was doing.

His concern for her touched her, and were it not for the tragedy of the situation, she would have been deliriously happy. She was happy, but in a sad way. The love blossoming between her and Liam sustained her during the early dark days following Ben's death.

Ginny remained dazed and quiet, and Eloise worried about her constantly. The doctor had come to check in on her, and said she was healthy as was the baby, and that Ginny would be fine. She was in shock.

Liam continued to work on the house, and was now busy updating the kitchen and bathroom given that Eloise had decided to live there.

Once they all moved on from this.

She didn't know how everything would turn out, it wasn't just her fear about what Ashleigh would say, but they were destined for many changes, a new baby being one of them.

Ford and Darcie came daily to see how they were. Darcie brought food, something that Eloise was especially grateful for.

She kept an eye on Ginny and went to work when she could. In doing both, she was often too exhausted to cook.

"We need to talk, but not here," Ford warned as soon as he'd seen Ginny. Her sister often spent the day on the sofa, watching TV, but often when Eloise looked in on her, Ginny's attention would be far away.

Alarm bells went off in Eloise's head. "Talk about what?" She couldn't handle any more drama in her life.

"Not here," Ford insisted.

She stuck her head into the living room. "I'm going out for a walk with Ford, Gin. I won't be long."

Ginny nodded her head.

"But I can stay, if you want," Eloise offered.

"I'll be fine." But Ginny didn't sound fine. Her voice was listless, her face sombre. Dark shadows stained the skin under her eyes. "I'll be fine," she insisted.

"I won't be long." She reluctantly left with Ford, walking out of the back yard and moving far away from the house. Eloise folded her arms, protecting herself from what she feared was more trouble.

Worry lines etched Ford's brow, and he paced around in front of her. "I knew."

"Knew what?" The poor man looked as if he was carrying the weight of a boulder.

"I knew there was someone else."

"When? How?"

"I was in a bar, and I saw him with someone. It was not long after the wedding was canceled. He might not have been with her, but it was only the two of them and they looked... familiar. Like they knew each other well."

Eloise feared that her heart couldn't take any more bad news. "How well? Did they look like they were together?"

Ford shrugged. "I can't tell. They weren't kissing or anything."

"Were they alone or with others?"

"It was just the two of them."

She tried to shake the image out of her head. The permutations and different reasons as to why Ben was with that woman then, and why he'd gone back to Ginny. And then he was in an accident with someone else in his car.

If the accident hadn't happened, they would never have known about the other woman. Had he been faithful to Ginny ever since he found out about the baby?

Nothing mattered now because Ben wasn't here. It would open a can of worms she would rather not deal with.

"I'm sorry." Ford looked the roughest she'd ever seen him. She wondered if there was something else going on with him. "How's your mom? And Maddie?"

"They're fine. Why?"

"You don't look so good."

"I was supposed to keep an eye on you both and I failed miserably."

"Don't be hard on yourself. You didn't fail us. This... everything that's happened is not your fault. You didn't fail us, so stop thinking like that. There are enough of us walking around feeling guilty. It's life, that's what this is. That's what has happened. Life. It sucks." Tension bunched up around her shoulders and she could feel the light reverberations of a throbbing headache. "I knew Ashleigh asked you and Darcie to keep an eye on us."

Ford lifted a shoulder and gave her an it-wasn't-my-idea look. "She was worried about you both, about leaving you to deal with everything, about not being here for Ginny after the breakup."

"And that's what scares me now. She was so worried then, what is she going to think now?"

"Is Ginny still insisting on keeping Ashleigh in the dark?"

"She doesn't talk much. She's so fragile, Ford. I'm scared to tip things further over the edge."

He swiped a hand over his face and let out a sigh. "It's hard to know what to do when you don't want to hurt anyone, but sometimes doing nothing can be the worst thing you can do."

He, like Darcie, wanted her to tell Ashleigh. "I have a lot going on right now. I will. I'll tell Ashleigh, soon. Soon. But I can't handle doing that right now."

"I understand. Let's get back inside. It's getting cold and it's getting late." He glanced over at the summer house. "Liam's doing more work on that place."

"I told him to." A question seemed to dangle on his lips.

"Why did you send him to me?" She was curious to hear his side of things.

"Because you needed someone to work on your place, and he's a good guy."

"He knew me from high school."

"Yeah?"

She didn't know whether to believe him. "You didn't know?"

"He might have mentioned it."

"You did know." She grew suspicious. "Did you play matchmaker?

Ford chortled but didn't give her an answer.

"Did you?" she demanded.

He slapped a hand to the side of his neck, as if he was about to make a confession. She'd suspected as much. "I didn't play matchmaker. Not for you. You're too picky and prickly."

"Thanks." The sarcasm was thick.

"You push men away! If I did it for anyone, I did it for him."

She hadn't been expecting this. "Did what for him?"

"I sent him to you because he was available, because his work is good, and he was more than capable of doing it. But I thought it might be good for him. I'm not sure if I was expecting anything to happen, but that man has suffered heartache. He hasn't dated in years, not since his girlfriend died."

Her indignation softened away. "He told me."

"He told you?" Ford winked at her. "He tends not to open up about that to anyone. Maybe you're not just 'anyone' to him."

Eloise stayed quiet, not wanting to divulge any more information than was necessary.

"But, if he knew you back in high school, and he remembered you … that can't be a bad thing, can it?" Ford cocked his head. "Seems to me that you like him, too."

"I don't not like him." That was all she was giving Ford.

She more than liked Liam.

More than.

CHAPTER 33

She'd been tense the entire time during the flight over.

When Ford had called her, with Darcie beside him, and told her that it would be 'good if she returned' goosebumps went up all over her skin.

Was this why Ford had wanted to come over earlier? No matter how much she pleaded with them to tell her, they wouldn't, adding the worrying line, "Don't call Eloise or Ginny. Just don't."

"You're scaring me," she'd told them, fearing the worst, even though her friends had told her that Eloise and Ginny were safe and well. She'd feared the worst. Illness. Kidnapping. Death.

She began to pack as soon as she hung up, and she bought a ticket for the next flight back.

When she came out of the arrival lounge and saw Ford and Darcie waiting for her, and the somber looks on their faces, she knew something was very, *very* wrong. She began to tremble.

"Aw, look at you, hon!" Darcie wrapped her arms around Ashleigh's bewildered body. She was rigid, her mind trying to make sense of everything.

"Someone's died." She stared at their faces, trying to read for clues.

They looked at one another, which was worse.

"Tell me now, or I swear I'm going to call home and ask them myself."

They'd taken her over to a row of empty seats, and sat her down, and then, while Darcie held her hand, and Ford watched, she heard things she couldn't wrap her head around.

Ginny was pregnant, and back with Ben, and Ben had been involved in a car accident and had passed away a week ago. She shivered, the shock of the situation settling in her belly like a kidney stone. There was so much to take, to absorb and make sense of. Her mind felt ready to explode.

"Say something, hon." Darcie poked her arm. "Ashleigh?"

Ford's voice was solemn. "Do you understand what we've told you?"

Her head felt heavy. Her body numb. Her friends would never lie about such a thing. She knew it had to be something serious for them to call her and demand she come home. But this?

"Ginny is pregnant?" she said, finally, trying to imagine her little sister who had been heartbroken after the wedding had fallen through.

Ford nodded.

"And it's Ben's?"

Darcie stroked her palms gently. "Eloise thinks it must have happened before they canceled the wedding. She's just over five months."

"Five months?" A blur of images chopped and changed in her head.

Ginny pregnant.

Ginny as a mother.

Ginny with a baby.

With Ben.

But not with Ben.

Not now.

Ben had died.

"Ginny must be heartbroken. I need to see her."

"They don't know you're coming," Ford told her.

"Eloise has had her hands full. She's so busy rushing from the shop to Ginny. That poor girl is exhausted," said Darcie. "You mustn't blame her for not telling you. Ginny has been difficult, before Ben came along and ... there's so much to tell you."

She stood up. All her happy memories of her vacation disintegrated. "Take me home."

It was too much on some days, and the only thing that kept her going was the relentless pressure.

With it just being her in the shop, along with Rachel and May, she was overwhelmed. Most of the workload fell on her because they couldn't do the dress alterations, or the accounts. Ashleigh dealt with a few things, but Eloise wished she wouldn't. She would rather her sister switched off completely and enjoyed her vacation.

They had never worked with this in mind. Between the three of them, they'd never anticipated that there might come a day when only one of them would be able to work.

What if, for some reason, none of them could work? What then? What would become of The Bridal Shop, the business their mother had so passionately and painstakingly started?

"Gin, do you want to have some soup today? There's some of Darcie's homemade cheese and tomato bread." She walked over to her sister who was lying on the sofa.

It hurt her to see Ginny so inactive. So lethargic. So broken.

She sat down beside her and stroked her hair. It was greasy and she hadn't brushed it in days. "Do you want me to wash your hair for you?"

Ginny shook her head.

"You don't want me to wash your hair or you don't want soup?"

"I don't want anything."

Eloise pinched her eyebrows, a sharp pain followed and then a sense of relief. She was watching her sister waste away, and none of this could be good for her or the baby, despite the doctor saying otherwise.

"You have to eat, Gin. You have to move. How about we go for a walk to the summer house and I can show you how it's coming along?"

"Don't want to."

"It's not good lying around all day." Her sister's face was pale. Her eyes still haunted by dark shadows. Eloise was in despair, not knowing how to do this. How to fix it.

She got up, having decided. "You're going to have the soup with some bread."

Ginny didn't move, didn't look at her or acknowledge her. Eloise sighed and went into the kitchen. She thought she heard the key turn in the lock and her insides froze as she turned and looked at the door.

It slowly pushed open, fear spiralling in her gut, her mind going blank.

Then Ashleigh stepped in.

Eloise burst into tears and ran towards her. "You're back." She hugged her so tightly, not letting her go. Ford and Darcie walked in behind her.

"Why didn't you tell me?" Ashleigh whispered, and from that Eloise knew that she knew.

She kept her arms around Ashleigh, soaking in the big sister comfort and support, acknowledging how much she had missed it. How much she needed it.

Ashleigh moved away first, then wiped her tears. "It's going to be okay. Okay?"

Eloise nodded.

"Where's Ginny?" Ashleigh asked, and looked as if she was about to go upstairs. Eloise grabbed her hand and led her into the living room.

Ginny was still staring out of the window, hugging a cushion as she lay on the sofa. Ashleigh gasped. "Ginny." And flew to her.

The next few moments were of gasps and cries, and hugs. She stayed away, letting Ashleigh and Ginny hug it out.

"It's not so bad, is it?" Darcie put her arm around Eloise's waist.

"Thank you."

"Wasn't my idea. It was Ford's. We told her when we picked her up from the airport."

She understood.

CHAPTER 34

*I*t was way after midnight, and Ginny had gone to bed.

Eloise and Ashleigh sat at the table.

Ashleigh kept yawning and ignored Eloise when she told her to get to bed but she insisted on being told everything.

"I'm sorry I didn't tell you sooner. I wanted to, I know I should have, I know it would have been the most sensible thing to do, but Ginny and I were at loggerheads with one another."

"They explained to me."

"They?"

"Darcie and Ford."

Ashleigh rested her forehead on her hands. She still looked gorgeous, despite the flight and probably not having slept for hours. Her hair was still sun kissed and she had the most glorious tan.

Eloise felt invisible next to her. "It was good of them to tell you. Brave. I'm thankful that they took matters into their own hands. I've been in a sort of limbo ever since Ben's fatal accident. Ginny's been like a zombie and I've been so worried."

"And still you didn't think to call and tell me yourself?"

Eloise started to explain, again, but Ashleigh put out her hand, halting her. "I didn't mean it. I didn't. I'm sorry. You're not to blame."

"There's more. I'm not sure how much you know." Eloise took a deep inhale. It seemed wrong to bring it up now that Ben had died.

Ashleigh's eyes narrowed. "More? What else?"

"There was someone else in the car. Thank goodness it wasn't Ginny, but it was a woman."

Ashleigh sat forward, her brow creasing with worry. "A woman? Who?"

"I don't know. But Ford mentioned to me that he'd seen Ben in a bar with a woman, months ago, before he and Ginny got back together. It was just the two of them. He couldn't tell if they were together or not. Anyway, she's okay. She'll be fine. Her injuries weren't fatal. She broke a leg."

Ashleigh slumped back in her chair, a slow gasp easing out of her. "That ... that ..." She shook her head. "I shouldn't speak ill of the dead."

"No."

"Well, this has happened, and we have to help put Ginny back together again. We have to be there for her now more than ever."

"Like always," Eloise agreed, feeling thankful that she no longer had to keep this to herself.

Ashleigh swiped a hand over her face, looking defeated. "I can't believe what has happened in the few months I've been away. I'm sorry I left you."

Eloise sat upright. "Please don't be. You needed to go, and I needed to grow up. I see now how much you do, Ash," she said softly, fighting to hold back the sob that threatened to burst forth from her throat. "I didn't realize the sacrifices you made, and how lazy me and Ginny used to be in the past, knowing you would step in when we slacked off. I appreciate you so much."

"What is this?" Ashleigh's voice had a wobble. "You're turning all soft and mushy. It's not like you."

"I've had to grow up and take responsibility. I was so awful to you. Didn't you want to slap me every time I rushed off to Beth's for another vacation or party?"

Ashleigh stared at her in amusement.

"I'm sorry for being such a pain in your side," Eloise continued, her chest bubbling up with emotion. Ashleigh's face softened. "I had no idea how much you do, and every time we dropped out of doing the weekend rota, you stepped in, because you had to, because you had no choice. Because we weren't reliable."

"Oh my word," Ashleigh gasped. "I should go away and leave you more often."

"Don't you dare!" Eloise cried, but quickly retracked. "You can go. You have to, seeing as you cut your trip so short."

"I was in Croatia and then I was supposed to go to Greece and Turkey, after that.."

"I'm sorry. Let's get through these next few months and then you can go back."

"I think it wouldn't have been worth my while being there at this time of the year. It's cold and the tourist places shut down, not that I always lived the tourist life. A few times I rented a place that had no tourists in the area at all. I got to see the real heart of the place."

"You can go back next year," Eloise offered. "Ford can maybe go with you."

Ashleigh stretched her arms above her head, then yawned. "I can't even think about next year."

"I guess not. There's a lot we have to deal with."

The funeral and visiting Ben's parents, and arrangements for the arrival of a new baby. Ashleigh looked somber. "I still can't believe that my little sister is having a baby. I can't believe she's going to be a mother."

"We get to be aunts," Eloise said, excitedly.

"Mom and dad would have been grandparents."

They leaned forward, holding hands across the table, as tears ran down their faces.

CHAPTER 35

Ford hadn't been himself.

Ashleigh had noticed an aloofness about him and put it down to his mother being ill, but she was grateful for his intervention in getting her to return home and she wanted to thank him. So she asked him to meet her at the diner.

She arrived before him, and felt anxious as she waited for him. It was new and unfamiliar, and something had changed between them. Maybe it was being apart for so long. She saw him first, as he walked in, and her heart did a backflip inside her chest. He was tall and good looking, and he looked casual yet sexy in his slacks and shirt.

Then he saw her, and walked over, but he didn't kiss her on the cheek, or hug her. He was cold, and distant, and she was uneasy.

She asked after his mother, and he told her that she was fine, getting frailer and older by the day. She asked about Maddie, and he told her that she was fine, too. He asked about Ginny and Eloise and how things were now that Ashleigh had returned. She answered him. But it all felt stilted. Like they were on a blind date and had no connection.

They sat across the table from one another, holding menus in their hands, but something hard and prickly filled the distance between them.

"I'm not hungry," he said, abruptly, surprising and shocking her at once.

"Oh. Uh..." She was hungry. She'd come hungry, because that was the whole point, to meet for lunch, and eat and talk and catch up. She'd missed him and she wanted to see him. When he'd picked her up from the airport, Ford had been distant then. His hug had been friendly, there was no passionate kiss, no holding her tightly, no expression of how much he'd missed her. Whether that was to do with the gravity of what he had to tell her, or because Darcie was also there, she didn't know but he didn't seem like the man she'd left back in the summer. "You don't want to have any lunch?" She attempted a laugh. "What shall we do, then? Because I'm starving. I saved myself for you." He seemed to miss the double entendre and looked at the menu now lying on the table.

"I think it would be good for us to take a break."

Shock coursed through her veins.

A break?

"Why?"

"Maybe we rushed into this." He moved the salt and pepper shakers around, as if he couldn't bring himself to look at her. "I feel that I might have rushed you into this. You might not be ready." He looked at her then, but the audacity of his statement made the hairs on her skin rise in indignation. "You can't make that assumption for me."

"I felt a distance between us when you were away."

She had an idea what he was getting at. "There was a distance between us, Ford. It's called the Atlantic Ocean."

He frowned, and she knew she'd sounded condescending.

"I was going to surprise you, by coming over. You must

have suspected that, but you made it perfectly clear you didn't want anyone to ruin your newfound freedom. It almost felt like you were suffocated by the idea of me going over."

"That's not… that's not entirely true." She scratched the skin behind her ear, feeling guilty, knowing that he wasn't wrong in his assumption.

"Eloise was the one who wanted me to go," Ford continued. "She wanted me to tell you about the situation at home. She was going out of her mind trying to do the right thing. Ginny was so stubborn, and Eloise urged her to tell you, but she didn't, so Eloise wanted me to be with you and tell you face-to-face, to make the news easier to bear. She didn't think it was fair to tell you over the phone."

This much she understood, but his decision perplexed her. "What has that got to do with us needing a break?"

He swiped his hand over his face as if he couldn't bring himself to say it.

"Ford." She leaned forward, anticipating the worst. Thinking that maybe he'd grown bored and tired of her. That rekindling a romance over two decades long no longer had the fire. That maybe someone else had come along …

"Did you meet someone?" he asked.

"What?" He'd knocked the air out of her lungs.

"Did you meet someone else? Because if you did, you just have to say it. Just be truthful."

She was incensed. "I didn't meet anyone! I mean, I met *people*." Now wouldn't be the time to tell him that she'd received many compliments and offers of drinks and dinner and goodness knows what else those men might have expected afterwards, but she'd declined them all. She wasn't interested in that. She wasn't interested in anyone else, because getting back with her first love meant the world to her.

Ford looked like an injured animal. "You like your freedom,

and I respect that. I understand that, because I know the burden you carry, the responsibility not only for the business but also for your sisters. But you made me feel like a commodity; as if I were someone, or something that you didn't need, not out there. I agreed with Eloise, that it would be best to tell you in person, and yes, it's true, I so badly wanted to see you because I missed you. I thought that maybe, for the first time in our lives, we could finally travel together, like we'd planned to all those years ago."

She put her hands together, feeling his hurt and seeing things from his point of view. "I didn't mean to treat you like a commodity." Her eyes welled up, and she was upset that he would think that. "I didn't mean to hurt you, Ford. I love you."

"You want to be free to do what you want, when you want, without anyone questioning you."

Her eyes widened and she blinked in shock. He'd remembered it verbatim. He'd stored those words away and held them against her. He'd made them mean something else, and not what she'd intended. "While I was out there! That's what I meant. It was a new way of being for me. Surely you can understand that?"

"I do understand. I love you, but maybe it's too soon. Maybe I pushed you into something, and maybe a part of you likes being single. I don't want to be the guy you feel you have to be with, when your heart isn't in it."

"That's not true!" She hadn't heard him properly. She'd wounded him. "So, what? That's it? You're breaking up with me?"

Ford shrugged and said nothing.

"Did you meet anyone?" she asked, her heart galloping like wild horses. He gave her a look full of longing and sadness, and it crushed her heart. "It's only ever been you. I loved Susan, and it's unfair of me to say it— because she's the mother of my child and we were married for years—but what I have with you is different. It's a whole other level of wonderful."

She loved this man. She loved this man so much and she was blessed that they had found one another again. She wasn't going to lose him a second time. "Then … don't do this, Ford. It doesn't make sense. W-we…" *We can work it out.* But she couldn't say it without bursting into tears. She was consumed by sorrow and worry, with everything going on, and she couldn't take any more bad news.

"Let's take a break, for now. There's too much going on."

"For now? What does that mean?" she cried, a tidal wave of sorrow washing over her. "We have Ben's funeral in a few days, and I need you, Ford. We all need you." A world without Ford? She couldn't get through these days without him. Not now that she was getting used to him being in her life.

"I'll always be here for you all."

She huffed out a gasp, forcing herself not to fall apart even as he had crushed her. "Do you really want to do this?"

"The world has gone crazy. I feel like maybe we all need a little time out."

CHAPTER 36

"**I** approve," said Eloise, shifting her hips on the new countertop that Liam had fitted in the kitchen, and on which she was now perched, with her legs wrapped around his waist.

"You like it?" he asked, his arms around her waist, as he stood, kissing her, and murmuring sweet nothings into her ears.

Making her hot and bothered, and happy. "Kiss me again," she murmured, not even opening her eyes. Liam pressed his lips against hers and took her breath away.

He was her safe and happy place, and where she went in the evenings. Ashleigh had seen him once or twice, when he'd come by to see Ginny. He stopped coming every day.

Eloise told him that Ashleigh was still taking everything in, and she didn't want to overwhelm her by telling her that she and Liam were together.

But the evenings. The evenings by the summer house were her favorite times of the day. The anticipation of seeing Liam, of being in his arms, made the days more bearable.

It helped that Ash was back on so many levels. No longer was Eloise alone, and she helped with Ginny, who was proving difficult, as she remained quiet and was a constant cause of worry for the sisters.

The kitchen was still a work in progress, but she wasn't worried about it. The house, like her, was in good hands, with Liam.

She groaned appreciatively against his lips, looking forward to when this was done, and she could move in. Yet another thing she had to tell Ashleigh.

"You'll come to Ben's funeral, won't you?" she asked, feeling the weight of the day which was fast approaching. "Ginny wants you to come."

"Are you sure? I didn't really know the guy."

"I need you. Ginny will need you. We don't have close family; it's just us and close friends. Darcie, and Ford and … and you."

"Then, I'll be there."

"Thank you." She pressed her face against his neck. "I'm not sure how much more of the bad stuff we can take."

His gaze bounced between her eyes. "I'll be there with you, every step of the way. I'll be there for Ginny, whatever she needs."

"Thank you."

They kissed again and she fell against his chest, inhaling the scent of him, the strength of him.

"Oh!"

She and Liam pulled away. Ashleigh hovered in the kitchen door, not daring to step in. She looked like a deer caught in the headlights, frozen for a split second, before she started to move back. "I... didn't mean to..."

Eloise disentangled herself from Liam and hopped off the counter, rushing to her sister because she could see she'd been crying. "What?" She grabbed Ashleigh's shoulders, fearing the worst.

The worst seemed to have no limit. "What?"

Ashleigh braved a smile, but her eyes were filled with sadness. "It's... nothing. I... I need to get back to Ginny. I'll start making dinner."

"Excuse me, ma'am," said, Liam, wanting to get past. Ashleigh was blocking his way.

"Sorry," Ashleigh sniffled and moved out of the way, but didn't look at Eloise. Something was clearly wrong. Eloise grabbed her hand and pulled her into the kitchen, safe in the knowledge that Liam had given them privacy. "Tell me now, Ash, and don't beat about the bush. I swear I'm going to have a heart attack if things don't let up for us soon."

"Ford broke up with me."

"What?" Eloise cried, as the air seemed to get sucked right out of her lungs. "*Why*? What possible reason did he have?"

She listened as Ashleigh recounted their conversation earlier, her voice wobbling as she tried not to burst into tears. "I love him. I love him and I don't understand why he did this."

But Eloise did understand. She'd seen Ford's face when he told her he had canceled his ticket to go over.

"You hurt him, Ash," she said softly, putting her arms around her sister and holding her.

"I didn't mean to." Ashleigh sniffled. "I didn't mean to."

Eloise pulled away, her arms still around her sister. "I know you might not have, but he took it that way."

"I don't want to break up. I love him."

Eloise sighed. She'd seen both sides of it, and she understood both Ashleigh and Ford. This was unlike Ford, though. "I think you broke his heart, Ash. He missed you so much, and me asking him to go to you was the excuse he needed."

Ashleigh moved away and swiped a hand over her face. "I feel broken."

"Come here." She hugged her sister again, her heart aching for her.

"What am I going to do?" Ashleigh whispered.

"Let's get through the next few days. Ginny needs us to get her through the funeral. Ford will be there. He's still a friend, our friend, and he will always be here for us."

"But I don't want him to just be my friend," Ashleigh sniffled.

"We'll sort it all out later. He just needs more time."

"Okay." Ashleigh nodded. "Okay. More time. He just needs more time."

"Ginny is home alone. We should go."

"You didn't think to tell me about your new romance?" Ashleigh asked as they walked back.

"I was going to, but things have been kinda crazy around here. I don't know if you noticed.

"I noticed."

CHAPTER 37

"Are you sure you can do this, Gin?" Eloise asked, placing a hand on her sister's arm. Ashleigh fussed around her, combing her hair.

They'd had to help her to get dressed. Ginny all in black, wearing a maternity dress that made it so obvious that she was pregnant. She looked paler than ever. Eloise exchanged looks with Ashleigh. They'd discussed it last night and this morning, about whether it would be wise for Ginny to go, but Ginny had been adamant that she wanted to.

Even Darcie had said she needed to go, to get closure.

Ginny looked like she'd been crying all night. "I have to go. It wouldn't be right if I stayed at home."

They hooked their arms in hers and prepared to leave the house.

"I want to say something." Ginny stopped in the hallway. "I know you all talk about it. I know most people in the town probably talk about it, but I'm going to hold my head up high today, because I want everyone to know that I'm not hiding. I know the rumors. I know he was in a car with someone that wasn't me, and I feel crushed and broken if I think about it for too long. He hurt me once, and then I let him hurt me again. I thought he had changed, but even I could see that something wasn't right. I had my suspicions but I so desperately wanted to believe that everything would work out, I ignored all the warning signs. I blame myself for being weak, so you both don't have to keep doing that."

Shock tasered through Eloise at what her sister had said, and she and Ashleigh quickly reassured Ginny that this wasn't true.

"Don't lie," said Ginny, eyeing them both in turn. "I know how you look at me. The I-told-you-so thoughts lurking behind your words."

"Ginny." Ashleigh stroked her arm, then tucked a stray lock behind Ginny's ear. "We were worried, I won't lie, but we don't think you're weak. You are stubborn and headstrong, and you've been dealt so many blows in your young life. It isn't fair. We know Ben hurt you, and we're angry about the things we're hearing, but Ben isn't here, and there's no use in badmouthing him."

"Yeah, Gin. We're here for you, and as much as it sounds cruel, we don't think about Ben much. We think about you and the effect all of this is having on you. We're worried about you and the baby."

"You don't have to worry about me. I've been lying like a sack of potatoes on the couch, but I've needed that time to get my head straight. My baby is my priority now and I have to think about that. I have to think about me. After today, I'm going to put this all behind me and make a new start."

"Okay." Eloise hugged her, and she and Ashleigh exchanged knowing looks. It wasn't going to be easy. Ginny would still have breakdowns as she moved closer to her due date, and even after that, when the baby had its first milestones.

There would be plenty of sadness and tears, but as long as they were together, they could cope with anything.

The doorbell rang and when they opened it, it was Darcie looking smart and regal in her black dress. She'd kindly offered to take them to the funeral. "Are you all ready?"

"Are we ready?" Eloise looked at Ashleigh and Ginny. Eloise was strong, and was aware that this would be a difficult day for Ginny, and also for Ashleigh who would be seeing Ford for the first time since the day they'd broken up.

"I'm ready," they said in unison, as they left the house to go to Ben's funeral.

CHAPTER 38

They were digging into a tub of Ben & Jerry's chocolate ice cream.

It was a much-needed reward for getting through the hard day.

Being in Ben's house, surrounded by his family and friends had been too much for Ginny to take in.

They hadn't stayed long.

Ginny had gone to bed as soon as they returned home late in the afternoon after the wake.

While Eloise and Ashleigh had kept an eye on Ginny, Eloise had also watched Ashleigh and Ford carefully.

He sat with them, as did Darcie, and to everyone else it must have seemed as if they were together. But Eloise noted the nuances. The expressions, the barely spoken words between them, and her heart ached for Ashleigh. Just like it did for Ford. These two people deserved to be together, and the fact that they now weren't was a tragedy.

They'd tried to get her to eat something, seeing as she hadn't eaten much all day, but Ginny refused. And because she looked so ashen and fragile, she and Ashleigh decided to let her go to sleep. Eloise felt so much better. Having someone to share her worries with was the only way to cope.

Ford and Darcie had been right in getting Ashleigh to return.

"It was nice to see Ford again." Eloise missed his daily presence at the house, when he would come to see how she and Ginny were coping. She hoped it wouldn't always be like this. That he wouldn't stay away and avoid them forever.

That at some point he would realize Ashleigh needed him and loved him, and he would forget what silly idea he had in his head.

"We were like strangers." Ashleigh scooped out a big spoon of ice cream and plopped it into her mouth.

"I don't want you two to be strangers."

"It's out of my hands." Ashleigh waved the spoon in the air, indicating that she was helpless to remedy the situation.

"It takes two to break up and make up."

A line appeared between Ashleigh's brows. "You didn't hear him that day. He was sad, and quietly angry."

"You can fix it." Eloise dug out another spoonful of ice cream. "You can visit the places you didn't get to see this time, and take Ford with you."

"And leave you and Ginny and the baby here?"

"I'll have Liam to help me," she said, brightly.

"You two are cute together."

"You approve?"

"Approve?" Ashleigh looked hurt. "Why would I not? And, who am I to approve or disapprove?"

"He grew on me." Eloise thought back to the day she'd first met him.

"Grew on you?"

"I wasn't looking for anything to happen, but, he just kinda grew on me."

"Like I said, you're cute together. He seems kind and nice. Trustworthy and reliable. I like that he checks in on Ginny."

"And me."

"And you." Ashleigh let out a long sigh. "I've forgotten how precious it is to have someone. To be half of a whole."

Eloise waved her empty spoon at her. "He'll come back. I know he will, and if he doesn't, you whisk him away to Europe."

"It's not going to be so easy." Ashleigh seemed to have the weight of the world on her shoulders.

"We'll figure something out, going forward." She looked deep in thought.

"We don't have long left," Eloise agreed. "We have to convert one of the rooms into a nursery and start buying—"

"I meant about the business."

"The business?" Eloise asked.

"It was like I'd been unchained and let loose," said Ashleigh. "Every day I woke up and I didn't have to go to the shop and take care of things. Having your own business is harder than going to work. At work, in a normal nine to five job, you can take it easy. You can talk to your friends, take longer for your lunch, start and finish at set times. If anything goes wrong, your boss has to deal with it. The business churns along because you're just one spoke in a wheel. With us, it's not like that. We are the business. It depends on us. It keeps us pinned here, and it keeps us shackled."

Hearing such strong words from Ashleigh shook Eloise. As she'd feared, her sister had come to enjoy the freedom. And now, with Ginny busy with her baby for the next year or more, it was down to the two of them.

If either of them wanted a small break, it would mean leaving the other one in charge of everything, and leaving them with a responsibility and burden that was too big for one person to carry alone.

"You and Liam could get married one day."

Eloise exploded into laughter, though her heart somersaulted in her chest. But … maybe it wasn't entirely impossible. "You're getting ahead of yourself," she said in her sternest voice.

"Am I?" Ashleigh raised an eyebrow. "Look at you, all glowing and happy. So uncharacteristically like the sister I left behind. Has Beth noticed a difference in you?"

"She thinks I'm avoiding her. She doesn't know about Liam, and I've been too busy to bring her up to date."

"You and Beth have been joined at the hip for years, and yet she doesn't know about you and Liam?"

"With everything going on, it's the last of my worries." Then, as Ashleigh became silent, she asked, "What did you mean about the business?"

"Maybe we sell it and move on?"

"You would think of selling mom and dad's business?"

"Mom wouldn't want us to be chained to it. We've run it as best as we can. Don't you want to live life and do things?"

She did, but she also enjoyed the good income they had from this. Her goals had changed. She no longer wanted to move away and work for anyone.

She wanted to stay here, and with some help, if Ashleigh wanted to move on, and if Ginny couldn't help anymore, she'd find a way to keep The Bridal shop going.

"I'm going to move into the summer house."

She waited for Ashleigh's reaction, but her sister's face was hard to read. "I had a feeling you would. Don't ask me why, but I've sensed a restlessness about you. I'm glad you're only moving across the field instead of to Hyannis Port."

"There's nothing for me in Hyannis Port."

The next day she went over to the summer house to see Liam.

He'd been expecting her, by the looks of things. By the way he'd set up a small table outside next to the patio chairs, with a small heater close by to keep them warm.

The furniture for the house would be arriving in the next few weeks, and she wasn't sure about when she would move in. With Ginny's baby due in a few months, it didn't seem fair to leave Ashleigh at home to take care of Ginny when the nights would be hard with a crying, hungry baby.

Maybe she'd wait a while.

"Hey." Liam scooped her up into his arms and she wrapped her legs around him again, as he took her inside, their lips sealed, arms around one another.

She needed this. Someone to belong to, someone who would soothe away the worries of the day.

"Thank you for yesterday," she said, in between kisses.

"Don't thank me for being by your side. I told you, I'm here for you, always …"

"And forever?" she asked, caught up in the sweet heat of their kissing, and not thinking as the words tumbled out. She looked at him, feeling unsure, hesitant, vulnerable.

"Forever, yeah. I would like that." He nuzzled her nose, before setting her down, still keeping his arms wrapped around her.

"But we'll take it slow," she cautioned, even as her heart was in free fall. Gazing into his eyes she lost herself in the burst of green and gold, felt something warm wash over her. A feeling that she wasn't alone. Something about Liam grounded her, and made her happier than she'd been in a long time.

He nodded. "Whatever you say."

"And you don't mind being with an older woman?"

"Are you older than me?" he asked, feigning surprise.

She punched him lightly on the chest. "You might not think it's a big deal now but …" She wanted to say that in years to come, he would notice, but before she could say another word, he pulled out his cell phone and took a selfie of them both, then showed it to her. "We look good together, no?"

She had to admit. They looked so good. So together. So much a couple. "We do."

"I'm falling for you, Elle, because of your heart, it's so much bigger than you think. And you're cute, and feisty, and … and I can't believe I got to be with the cheerleader from high school. Who'da thought?" Before she could answer, he gave her a kiss that made her toes curl. "I don't care about the age. Okay?"

She felt dizzy, from his kiss and his closeness, from his words and his wisdom. She was giddy with the thought of what a future with this man might mean. "Okay."

"I've set up outside, seeing that we have no decent furniture inside."

"I saw." She didn't care where they were, as long as they were together.

"How was Ginny last night?" he asked.

"Not in a good place at all." She stared at him wistfully. "We just need her to get strong again. That girl has had more than her share of knocks. She deserves a break. I'm always so scared and worried for her."

"Hey." He put his finger under her chin and turned her face towards him. "She will be fine. You know why? Because you are an amazing sister to her. You took great care of her, even with her mood swings and everything else that was going on. You had so much to deal with. I could always see the stress on your face when you'd come over. Seems to me that you always put your family first, Elle, and Ginny knows that, even if she doesn't say it to you in those words."

"Elle?" she asked, loving the sound of his new nickname for her.

"Mind if I call you Elle? Not because I'm too lazy to say Eloise, but because only I can call you that."

She smiled. "Do I get to call you El, on account of your first initial?"

"You can call me whatever you want." He leaned forward and pressed his lips to hers. A surge of heat shot through her, a mixture of desire and longing.

"I like calling you Liam."

He nodded.

"You come a very close second to my family," she told him.

"Yeah?"

"Yes." Because the only person she felt close to after her sisters, was this man. He hugged her closer to him, and in a moment where time seemed to have stopped, they remained like that, standing chest to chest, hearts beating as one.

Eventually, he took her outside where he placed a blanket over them once they'd sat down. The warm heat from the heater took the edge off an otherwise cold day.

"Ford and Ashleigh seemed distant yesterday," Liam commented.

She told him about their breakup. "Ford says it might be good for them to take a break."

Liam looked pensive. "He hasn't said a word to me about it."

"Don't ask him. He just needs some time to figure it all out."

"His mom isn't too well."

"That can't be easy." She wondered if that might have added to the stress that Ford was currently going through. This wasn't a time for Ford to be alone. Liam had helped her, and she was going to push Ashleigh to make it up with Ford if the man was too stubborn to do anything about it himself.

She looked around her. "I wanted to move in here quickly but now I think it might not be for a few months. I can't leave Ashleigh by herself to take care of the baby and Ginny during the nights."

"You'll do the right thing, because you always do." He reached for her hand, and gently stroked the back of it with his thumb. The warm, comforting feeling stirred deep-buried emotions inside her.

She loved this. Loved sharing her day with Liam, loved having him around. Loved being one half of a whole.

Who knew what else the world had in store for her and her sisters? At least Liam would be there to help her through it.

She'd found a man she was willing to risk her heart with.

Although, had she found him, or had he found her?

A slow smile spread across her lips. Shifting back against her chair, still holding hands, they sat in silence, watching the gentle lull of the ocean. She could see herself doing this, with him, many years into the future.

At last, she'd finally found what she'd been looking for—to be loved by a good man, and to belong.

Everything she'd wanted had been here, in Whisper Falls, all along.

Thank you for reading THE SUMMER HOUSE! I hope you enjoyed reading Eloise's story. Ginny's story will be next.

SIGN UP FOR MY NEWSLETTER to find out when new books release:
http:/www.siennacarr.com/newsletter

. . .

Looking for something to read while you wait? I have another series, STARLING BAY, which is set in a small coastal town and features many memorable characters. These are standalone romances with each featuring a different couple, although these friends and acquaintances are all interconnected and appear in each other's books.

WINTER'S KISS is the first book and it's the story of a jaded widow, a difficult teen, a sexy gift store owner and an adorable Great Dane!

She's the city girl from Boston. He's the gift shop owner from the bay. Their worlds were never meant to collide.

Merry Nicholls loathes Christmas. The season is full of bad memories because of her husband's sudden death. At her mother's insistence, Merry reluctantly visits Starling Bay with her surly daughter and her Great Dane in tow.

But all chances of a restful period go out of the window when her dog crashes into a gift shop, causing mayhem and angering the handsome shop owner.

I appreciate your help in spreading the word, including telling a friend, and I would be grateful if you could leave a review on your favorite book site.

Thank you and happy reading!
Sienna

BOOKLIST

The Rose Sisters:
The Bridal Shop
The Summer House

Starling Bay books:
Whirlwind Kisses
Winter's Kiss
Maid for Him
Love Letters
Escape to Starling Bay (Books 1-3)
From Faking to Forever
Winter's Vow
Guarded Hearts
Table for Two
A Bouquet of Charm
Christmas Wish

ACKNOWLEDGMENTS

I would like to thank my amazing group of proofreaders who check my manuscript for errors, typos and inconsistencies.
I am eternally grateful for their help and support:

Marcia Chamberlain
Dena Pugh
Carole Tunstall

I would also like to thank Tatiana Vila of Vila Design for creating the awesome cover.

ABOUT THE AUTHOR

Sienna Carr is the sweet romance pen name for an author who has been writing romance since 2013. She lives in the UK with her husband, three children, and a parrot.

Connect with Me

I love hearing from you – so please don't be shy!
You can email me at: sienna@siennacarr.com

Newsletter | Goodreads | Bookbub | Website

bookbub.com/authors/sienna-carr